Bello:

hidden talent rediscovered!

Bello is a digital only imprint of Pan Macmillan,
established to breathe new life into previously published,
classic books.

At Bello we believe in the timeless power of the imagination,
of good story, narrative and entertainment and we want to use
digital technology to ensure that many more readers
can enjoy these books into the future.

We publish in ebook and Print on Demand formats
to bring these wonderful books to new audiences.

About Bello:

www.panmacmillan.com/imprints/bello

About the author:

www.panmacmillan.com/author/andrewgarve

Andrew Garve

Andrew Garve is the pen name of Paul Winterton (1908–2001). He was born in Leicester and educated at the Hulme Grammar School, Manchester and Purley County School, Surrey, after which he took a degree in Economics at London University. He was on the staff of *The Economist* for four years, and then worked for fourteen years for the *London News Chronicle* as reporter, leader writer and foreign correspondent. He was assigned to Moscow from 1942/5, where he was also the correspondent of the BBC's Overseas Service.

After the war he turned to full-time writing of detective and adventure novels and produced more than forty-five books. His work was serialized, televised, broadcast, filmed and translated into some twenty languages. He is noted for his varied and unusual backgrounds – which have included Russia, newspaper offices, the West Indies, ocean sailing, the Australian outback, politics, mountaineering and forestry – and for never repeating a plot.

Andrew Garve was a founder member and first joint secretary of the Crime Writers' Association.

Andrew Garve

THE
MEGSTONE
PLOT

First published in 1956 by Collins

This edition published 2012 by Bello
an imprint of Pan Macmillan, a division of Macmillan Publishers Limited
Pan Macmillan, 20 New Wharf Road, London N1 9RR
Basingstoke and Oxford
Associated companies throughout the world

www.panmacmillan.com/imprints/bello
www.curtisbrown.co.uk

ISBN 978-1-4472-1582-0 EPUB
ISBN 978-1-4472-1581-3 POD

Visit **www.panmacmillan.com** to read more about all our books
and to buy them. You will also find features, author interviews and
news of any author events, and you can sign up for e-newsletters
so that you're always first to hear about our new releases.

Chapter One

It all began with a chance encounter on a murky evening in November, 1954. I had just left the office and had stopped in Whitehall to buy a paper. As I turned away from the stand I felt a detaining hand on my arm and a man said, "Surely it's Clive Easton?"

I knew his face, but for a second I couldn't place him.

"Dunoon!" he said—and then it all came back. His name was Walter Cowley. He'd had a job during the war advising on low-temperature equipment for the Navy, and I'd run into him on the Clyde when the H95 was being fitted out for an Arctic mission. It had been a brief and superficial acquaintance, but as I remembered it he'd been a tolerable drinking companion in a lean week, and I wasn't too appalled at seeing him again.

It was cold for standing about, so I suggested we should pop into the Red Lion and have a chat. He obviously wanted to talk, but he said his wife was expecting him and wouldn't I go along and have a drink with them at home—it wouldn't take more than three or four minutes in a taxi, and he knew she would be delighted to meet me. I'd have preferred the pub, but he pressed me and I couldn't decently refuse.

On the way, we exchanged our bits of news. I told him I'd been working at the Admiralty as a sort of back-room boy since the war, and that I hadn't married, and that I was living in a flat near Sloane Square. He told me that after leaving the Service he'd gone back to his refrigerating plant business, and that he was doing fairly well on the export side and traveled abroad a good deal. He said he'd been married for five years, but hadn't any family. That was as far as we'd got when the taxi drew up outside a detached house in a quiet street off the Royal Hospital Road.

He opened the door with his latch key and called to his wife that he'd brought a friend home with him. Then he took me into a large, expensively furnished drawing room, and asked me what I'd like to drink. While he busied himself with the bottles, I had a good look at him. He was much as I remembered him—a short, slight man, good looking in a dapper sort of way, with mild, accommodating eyes—but he was beginning to show his age, which I reckoned was about forty-five. His slicked-down hair was thin and graying, and his face in repose was faintly anxious.

I was prepared for his wife to be harassed and forty-five, too—which made her actual appearance all the more breath-taking. She wasn't a day over thirty, and she was lovely. She was tall and rather statuesque, with a mass of dark brown hair that waved back from a round forehead. She had high cheekbones and sleepy-looking eyes and a full, sensual mouth. Her movements were slow and she spoke with an attractively insolent drawl. She had the poise and grace of a leopardess and I thought she was superb. I couldn't imagine how an insignificant little man like Cowley had ever managed to acquire her.

He introduced me flatteringly, undeterred by my protests. I hadn't realized until then how great an impression I must have made on him in those few days at Dunoon, or how closely he'd followed my wartime career afterwards. He insisted on presenting me as a romantic hero—"Clive Easton, D.S.O."—"One of the few R.N.V.R. chaps to be given a submarine command"—"Sank the *Wilhelm II*." His wife—her name was Isobel—regarded me appraisingly during this panegyric, and then gave me a slow, appreciative smile. I didn't think it was solely on account of my war record.

"Well, I'm sure you two want to talk about old times," she said. "I'd better efface myself." She took her glass and removed herself to a divan a few feet away and arranged herself carefully. She was about as inconspicuous as a siren on a rock.

Cowley kept the conversation seesawing around Dunoon for quite a time. From the way he talked, it might almost have been supposed that we'd been close friends. He took absurd pleasure in recalling quite trivial incidents, and he worked his way conscientiously through a list of casual acquaintances whose existence I'd almost forgotten. His anxiety to extract every possible scrap of reflected glory from our brief association was pathetic. He even asked me earnestly if the special boots he'd recommended for the Arctic trip had been all right, as though the chief danger off the North Cape had been frostbite and he'd personally averted it.

It was all dreadfully tedious, and I could only suppose I must have been pretty tight when I'd found his company tolerable. I'd have been on my way in no time if it hadn't been for the Gioconda on the divan. She fascinated me. Her husband was too busy talking about subzero temperatures to notice her provocative pose, but it hadn't escaped me. I felt sure she was trying to put ideas into my head. It was a stimulating thought—and the longer I watched her the more certain I became. Every time our eyes met, which was often, the room seemed filled with unspoken invitation. Her smile was outwardly cool and detached, but I wasn't taken in. Unless I was very much mistaken, she was as detached as a bit of plutonium that's just going to form a critical mass with another bit and blow everything to blazes. I recognized the symptoms.

The Dunoon topic flagged at last, and Cowley turned the conversation to the sinking of the *Wilhelm II*. I gave him a short account of that overpublicized exploit, conscious all the time of his wife's quizzical gaze. Then he got me to tell him about the successful gun action off the Norwegian coast that had gained me the bar to my D.S.O. As I finished that story, and he rose to refill our glasses, Isobel said, "Well, you certainly have had some adventures, Commander! I don't know how you could bear to be shut up in one of those things—they sound terribly uncomfortable."

"It was an uncomfortable war," I said.

"But you talk as though you actually liked being in them."

"Oh, submarines have their points. . . . For one thing, you're not being pushed around by other people all the time—once you've reached your billet, you mostly make your own decisions. And there's nothing quite as thrilling as hunting and being hunted. Pitting your wits against the other man's, with everything at stake."

"You obviously enjoy danger."

"It fills a gap—gives one an illusion of significance. Life seems quite worth while when there's a good chance it may come to an end at any moment—not that I claim that as a novel idea."

"Do you mean it doesn't otherwise?"

"Oh, it's all right as long as you have good health and sharp appetites and avoid all serious thought!" I said.

She laughed. "You must find it very dull now, working in an office."

"That's an understatement. We all wanted quiet jobs just after the war, of course, but it was only reaction, and the feeling didn't last. It's about time I made a change, as a matter of fact, but it isn't easy to know what to change to."

"Surely you can think of *something* exciting to do?" she said. From the way she looked at me, I felt certain it wasn't work she had in mind. I'd been right—she was just a primitive.

I found it difficult to concentrate after that, and very soon I got up to go. They both came to the door with me, and Cowley said how glad he was that we'd run into each other and how much he'd enjoyed our talk. Isobel said she hoped they'd see more of me. I said I hoped so too, and for a moment our eyes met in complete understanding. Cowley didn't know it, but we'd virtually made an assignation, with only the date left open.

It was an exhilarating thought. I'd been telling myself for some time that I ought to start a new affair, and this one promised to be something rather special. I was eager to get the date fixed, but I didn't want to risk spoiling everything by being too impetuous. A little more reconnaissance was clearly called for, and the first move seemed to be to return the Cowleys' hospitality and find out a bit more about their setup. I had to go up to Glasgow for a few days in connection with the project I was working on, but as soon as I got back I rang them up. Walter Cowley answered the phone, and he said they'd be delighted to come in for a drink the next evening.

Just before they were due to arrive, I had a call from him. His wife, he told me, had suddenly developed a bad headache and had had to go to bed. He was very apologetic. For a moment I wondered if I'd taken Isobel too much for granted—if I'd misread the signs. I said I was sorry to hear about his wife, but wouldn't he come along for a quick drink anyway. He jumped at it.

It turned out to be a most useful meeting, and I decided it wouldn't have been beyond Isobel to arrange things just that way. Cowley talked at length about his business, and it emerged that he was going off to Amsterdam on the following Monday and would be away for three or four days. I said I thought he and his wife were very fortunate being able to travel around together mixing business with pleasure. He shook his head ruefully and said that Isobel rarely went with him on winter trips unless it was to somewhere very warm, which hardly ever happened. He wished she would, because it couldn't be much fun for her staying in that house by herself, and she often complained of being lonely! I said if he liked I'd take her out to dinner one evening, and he thought that was a splendid idea. He seemed genuinely concerned that she should have a good time, and was naïvely grateful.

On the Monday evening I rang her up and said I hoped her headache was better. She laughed and said she was fine. I asked her if she'd care to dine with me on Tuesday, and she said she'd love to. It couldn't have been simpler.

I called for her just before seven, and we went to a very new, very chi-chi little place in Chelsea where the food was good and the waitresses were mostly ballet dancers resting and the clientele was headline stuff. We had *scampi* and *coq au vin* and a bottle of Chablis, and kept the talk frothy and frivolous, with sexy overtones, until I couldn't bear to stay there any longer.

I took her home just after nine, and she asked me in for a drink. I dismissed the taxi and followed her into the drawing room. She said "Whisky?" and I said "Thanks!" She poured out a shot, and I stood behind her and slid my hands under her arms and over her breasts and kissed the back of her neck. She was trembling so much that the whisky spilled. Suddenly she turned and flung her arms round me, pressing her body against mine. I hadn't made any mistake. We were birds of a feather, all right—both predatory, and both eager prey. She said, "Do we *really* want a drink?" and I said I didn't. I pulled her down onto the divan and began to make love to her. After a while she said, "I know a more comfortable place than this," and we went upstairs.

I woke from a short, deep sleep to find the bedside light on and Isobel regarding me impassively across the pillow.

"Hullo!" she said. "Do we know each other?"

"We should!" I said. I looked at my watch, and it was nearly three o'clock. We'd had quite a session. "I suppose I ought to be getting home now."

"If you think you can make it."

I laughed. "What I see of you is feminine enough, but you've a crude, masculine sort of mind."

"So I've been told."

I stirred and stretched. "You know, that was even better than I expected."

"Not bad," she agreed.

"Who was it said that every man dreams of a beautiful woman who is both fastidious and shameless?"

She gave a complacent smile.

I slid out of bed and began to dress. "I can tell you one thing," I said. "If I were your husband, I'd never travel."

"If you were my husband, darling, I'd travel with you."

"He really is an odd chap, isn't he?"

"He's devoted to me."

"I suppose he trusts you."

"He hasn't any reason not to."

"You mean he hasn't found you out yet."

"That's what I mean."

"What do you really think about him?"

"I try not to think about him at all. He bores me to death." She reached for a cigarette and lit it.

"I suppose you married him for his money?"

She regarded me for a moment quite unemotionally. Then she said, "Not exactly. I married him for his prospects."

"Well, they don't seem to have turned out too badly."

"Yes and no."

"Oh? You must have been aiming high."

"I always aim high."

"Expensive house, nice furniture—masses of clothes, I don't doubt . . ."

"Oh, yes—and my own car in the garage . . ."

"Money to burn, in fact."

"That's where you're wrong. Money for a humdrum, conventional existence with Walter—that's all. Never enough for a fling without him. Comfort, but no freedom. And even the comfort's precarious. The house is mortgaged, the furniture and the car aren't paid for, the business is short of capital. The stupid little man can only just make ends meet. He's a flop."

"What did you think he was going to be—a tycoon?"

"I hoped he'd make real money."

"He wouldn't ever have looked that way to me."

"Well, I wasn't too sure about it, but there seemed a chance, and anyway he was the best prospect at the time. I had to take what there was—I wasn't all that far up the ladder myself. Besides, he had a lot more drive and energy five years ago."

"You surprise me!"

"Oh, you've a single-track mind. It's nothing to do with me—it's just that he worries all the time. He lives on bismuth and aspirin and complains he can't sleep. He's a crock. He'll never get anywhere."

"Well, he's not the only pebble on the beach. Why don't you look around again? I imagine you could take your pick by now."

She shook her head. "Changing husbands advantageously is even more difficult than changing jobs. For one thing, we don't mix in the right circles. Walter only knows dreary people with dreary incomes like his own, and it's not easy for a married woman to go scouting around by herself. I have to be discreet—after all, I can't afford to throw away dirty water before I've found any clean, can I?"

I grinned. "Okay, I'll let myself out quietly."

"You'd better!"

"And I'll keep my eyes open for a likely millionaire. I'm afraid I'm not going to be much use to you. All I can offer is an unproductively distant connection with the peerage."

"Really?"

"Oh, yes—didn't Walter tell you? I'd have expected him to. The twelfth Earl of Colhousie was my granduncle—or is it great-uncle? I can never remember which."

"Doesn't that make you something?"

"Only a poor relation. I ran through all that was left of our part of the family fortune before the war—and you know what civil servants get."

"Oh, well, never mind, darling," she said. "Money's nice, but it isn't everything—we mustn't be sordid." She smiled. "At least we're going to have a lot of fun."

Chapter Two

As things turned out, though, we had regrettably little fun. Little in quantity, that is. I spent two more nights of abandonment with her, and then Walter returned, and our affair came to a full stop before it had got properly under way. I'd taken it for granted we should find some means of continuing to see each other while he was around, but to my surprise and dismay Isobel turned down all my schemes as too risky. In spite of her contemptuous talk about the comforts her husband had provided, she actually had a very shrewd appreciation of their value, and what she'd said about not throwing away dirty water had been much more than an amusing piece of bitchiness. Her appetites were strong once they were aroused, but they were far from being out of hand, and in her calculated order of priorities security came first. She was absolutely determined to take no chances, and for her that meant postponing our next meeting until Walter went away again. I thought her attitude cold-blooded, but nothing I could say would make her change her mind. She was a woman of character, even though it might be bad character. For me, the whole situation was intolerably frustrating. I wasn't in love with her, and I didn't suppose I'd ever want her for keeps, but I found her madly desirable, and I'd have given almost anything for a long lease.

I continued to see her fairly often in Walter's company. It was a tantalizing way of meeting her, but better than nothing, and I thought it might make things easier for us later on if I consolidated my position as a friend of the family. There was no difficulty about that, because Walter was always delighted to see me. I still found him unbelievably dull, but he was such a simple, friendly, good-natured chap that I couldn't really dislike him. I merely despised him. He must have had considerable skill in his own line of business, of course, or the Admiralty wouldn't have used him during the war and he wouldn't have got on as well as he had done since—but domestically he was a pinhead. After five years of marriage to Isobel, he was still blindly and uncritically proud of his lovely wife, and his one aim in life was to please her and appear well in her eyes. I simply couldn't imagine his being suspicious of her.

The way Isobel handled him was an object lesson in female duplicity. *I* knew what she thought about him, but he didn't. Her attitude towards him—at least when I was around—was invariably one of easygoing tolerance, and I'm sure he never sensed the heartless indifference underneath. Again, her policy was calculated—she'd made up her mind not to rock the boat as long as she was in it, and she stuck to that. She was sustained, no doubt, by her lingering hope that something better would turn up in the end, but I still thought her restraint and patience astonishing.

Over the weeks, I came to know a good deal about her way of life. She was, of course, blatantly selfish and utterly spoiled. She didn't have to do a stroke of work, in or out of the house, and she had no responsibilities or obligations of any sort. At the same time, she was by no means an indolent person. Her air of languor, like her drawling voice, was pure affectation, and when it came to amusing herself she was extremely active. She loved driving, and she was always running around town in the fast little Sunbeam Talbot that Walter had bought for her. She was a keen personal shopper, a source of steady profit to her *coiffeur*, a frequenter of dress shows, and a regular luncher-out. She managed to see most of the new films and plays, usually by herself at matinees. In the evenings, to save herself trouble and to spare herself the monotony of Walter's undiluted company, she generally got him to take her out to dinner. By and large, she must have been costing him a small fortune, and I could well understand his anxious expression.

She was, I soon realized, a very self-contained woman, as well as a self-centered one. She regarded most personal relationships as a mere nuisance unless there was some chance they might be useful to her. She certainly had no close women friends, which perhaps wasn't surprising. If she had relatives, she didn't talk about them—in fact, apart from that one remark she'd let slip about not having been far up the ladder when she'd met Walter, she never referred to her past at all. My own hunch was that she'd groomed herself out of a pretty squalid background. If so, that would explain the fierceness of her resolve to hold onto all the ground she'd won and her exaggerated caution over our affair.

On all other matters she was extremely candid. In spite of that—or perhaps because of it—I never felt at this time that I knew her really well. Our exchanges were cynical and brittle and all on the surface. I suppose that even then I suspected hidden depths and latent qualities or I wouldn't have been so intrigued by her, but she certainly gave no outward indication of them. She rarely showed much feeling, and I sometimes had the impression that a whole range of human emotions had been left out of her make-up. Her face, it was true, would register expressions like sympathy and pity on appropriate occasions, but I doubted whether anything was happening inside her. It seems an odd thing to say about a woman whose body was so warmly voluptuous and passionate, but she often struck me as rather a cold fish.

That didn't mean, of course, that she was dull. On the contrary, she had a lively, agile mind, and her conversation was almost always bright and amusing. She had plenty of leisure to read the papers and keep up to date with the news, and the sustained interest she took in everything that was going on in the world was uncommon in a woman. She certainly knew more about the latest celebrities and current books and crime and social scandal and even politics than her work-sodden husband, and she liked talking about them. No doubt the tightest bond between us was the looseness of our morals, but the fact that I could enjoy seeing her even with Walter around showed that there was something else besides. I never pretended to myself that she was a *nice* person, but she'd certainly have made an entertaining and satisfying companion on a world trip. That millionaire didn't know what he was missing!

It seemed ages before Walter went away again, and when he did it was for an exasperatingly short time. He was to travel up to Carlisle on the night train and return the next evening. Isobel told him it was bad for his health to do everything in such a rush and urged him to take an extra day, but he said he had to get back for a board meeting. She drove him to Euston and saw him safely off, and just before twelve I walked round to the house and slipped in quietly by the door she'd left ajar.

We had a wonderful reunion; so wonderful that I could hardly bear to think of the opportunities we'd been wasting, and were going to waste, because of her stubbornness.

"It's a pity," I said, as we lay side by side in the dark afterwards, "that you can't persuade Walter to go somewhere a long way off, like South Africa or India. Surely he could work up some export business there?"

"It wouldn't do us much good, darling. He'd be certain to fly, and he'd be back in a week."

"A week's a week."

"M'm!—yes—but I'm afraid it isn't very likely to happen, he's got too much on his plate already. . . . Never mind, he'll probably be going to Paris in the new year. We can look forward to that."

"What about in between?"

"You'll have to make do with your other girl friends."

"They seem insipid after you."

"They can't possibly be as insipid as Walter! I don't like the setup, either—but what can I do about it?"

"I've told you—lots of things. You could pop into my flat at lunch times, you could visit imaginary acquaintances on week ends, you could take up evening classes and cut them and have your lessons with me! There are dozens of ways."

"It's no good, Clive. Sooner or later we'd slip up, and he'd find out. It always happens. And then he'd divorce me."

"Nonsense! He'd forgive you, and we could start all over again."

"Well, I'm not going to risk it—even a worm will turn. He's my meal ticket, don't forget."

"You could eat less."

"It's not a thing to joke about! Suppose he did divorce me, where would I be? You know you couldn't support me."

"Not in the manner to which you've been accustomed, that's certain. Not unless I won a football pool or something."

"Ah, now you're talking ...! One of those very big ones, darling—wouldn't it be gorgeous?"

"Would you come away with me then?"

"Of course I would—if it was big enough. Just think!—we'd be able to get out of this ghastly climate—we could live in the sun—we could go to all the exciting places and be together all the time, and I'd never have to see Walter again. What a heavenly prospect!"

"I'll make a point of filling in my first coupon tomorrow!"

She laughed. "It won't work—I've tried it. You do them for three months and then get thirteen and eightpence."

"Well, I don't know any other way of making big money—not honestly."

"Do you have to be so fussy?"

"Or dishonestly, for that matter. I wouldn't have the least idea where to begin."

"Surely it's just a question of getting to know the right people?"

"You mean the wrong people—and that's the snag. It's only the right people that I do know."

"Then you should broaden your horizons. . . . I thought you were going to look for a new job, anyway."

"It wouldn't help. In the sort of job I'd really like to do, I'd only meet splendid chaps who didn't care about money."

"What sort of job?"

"Oh, joining some expedition—sailing a small boat round the north of Russia to the Pacific—mapping the lower Himalayas ... Crazy things! I'm probably past it by now, anyway."

"At thirty-eight, darling? Don't be silly."

"Well, not physically, perhaps, but I can't see myself making the effort, all the same. I shall probably stick around at the Admiralty now until I draw my pension."

"I don't know how you can bear it. What do you *do* there, anyway?"

'It's very hush-hush."

"Really?"

"Oh, yes, top secret!"

"You don't mean to say you're one of those atomic people?"

"*I'm* not, but atoms come into it. I sit in as the practical man—years of wartime experience, that sort of thing. . . ."

"I thought you said the work was dull. It doesn't sound dull."

"You'd be surprised! It couldn't be more humdrum. The slight cloak-and-dagger atmosphere is entirely bogus—nothing exciting or stimulating ever happens at all. There's so much paper work you don't even have time to resign. Actually, the whole thing's run by a top civil servant who could just as well be in the Treasury. Good chap in committee, you know. We practically live round a table. And the secrecy part's just nonsense, of course."

"Why?"

"Well, it's so unnecessary. For one thing, what we're doing has been done already by the Americans—our idea's only a development, and by the time we've perfected it, if we ever do, it'll be hopelessly out of date. Submarines are obsolete anyway. There'll be no sizable ports left undestroyed if there's another war, so there'll be no shipping to speak of, so why have submarines? They can't do anything that aircraft can't do better. When the security people behave as though the fate of the world depends on our project, it just makes me want to laugh."

"Perhaps you're underrating it, darling. I expect the Russians would be glad enough to know all about it."

"Oh, I dare say they'd be mildly interested—but then all govermnents are crazy."

"Why not try selling the secret to them? I expect it would pay better than football pools."

"What!—and have to live in Tomsk for the rest of our lives? No thanks!"

"Some people seem to think it's worth while."

"They don't do it for money—they're sold on communism. I'm only sold on you."

"Still, there must be *some* money in it. Look at that man

Henderson—he doesn't seem to have had any politics at all. Why did he disappear if he wasn't well paid for it?"

"He was rather a special case. After all, nobody really knows much about what happened to him. He could have been kidnaped."

"The papers seem to take it for granted that he went of his own accord."

"Yes, but you know what newspapers are. They'd have a nasty shock if he suddenly turned up again and could prove that he'd been knocked on the head and carried off against his will. He'd make a fortune out of damages."

"Would he really?"

"But of course. There could hardly be a worse libel than saying a man was a traitor when he wasn't."

"What do you call a fortune?"

"Oh, I don't know—he couldn't expect to go on collecting from paper after paper indefinitely, of course, but I wouldn't be surprised if he'd be able to knock up forty or fifty thousand pounds altogether. A useful lump sum, anyway—*and* tax free."

Isobel laughed in the darkness, "Well—there's your way out, darling! All you've got to do is seem to disappear and then turn up again, and we'll be able to go straight off to California."

"What a fascinating idea!"

"Isn't it? I'd love to be the mistress of a wronged man to whom full restitution had been made!"

I switched on the bedside lamp and began to look around for my clothes. "The trouble is, no one would realize I'd disappeared. They'd merely think I was at some conference. The Admiralty's an awfully big organization."

"Well, naturally you'd have to draw attention to the fact."

"Leave a message, you mean?—'Am disappearing today—please notify press'?"

"No, idiot, you'd have to lay a false trail. Do something suspicious."

"Like what?"

"Oh, mislay some secret papers, so that everyone thought you'd made off with them."

"Why would they think I'd made off with them? It's happening every day and no one gives it a thought. It might be months before anyone even noticed."

"Not if they suspected you, darling. You'd have to be seen going into the Soviet Embassy or something—for an innocent reason, of course."

"Like collecting material for an article on the ballet, I suppose . . . ? You'll have me in Dartmoor, not California."

"Well, perhaps not the Soviet Embassy, but you could easily do something that looked compromising but wasn't. Or send someone a message that was really quite innocent but didn't seem to be."

"It sounds quite an assignment to me. . . . Anyway, where would I disappear to?"

"Oh, somewhere nice and comfortable—you could give yourself an extra holiday that way."

"There'd be a bit of explaining to do afterwards, wouldn't there?"

"Not really—you'd simply come back after a few weeks, looking bronzed and fit, and say you were very sorry but you'd been suffering from loss of memory in Bournemouth."

"That's pretty corny, I must say. . . . Do you mind if I use your hair brush?"

"Why not, darling, you've used everything else I've got. . . . Anyway, I'm sure people have done that before."

"That's why it's corny."

"Well, there are other ways, if you're so particular. . . . You could get some accomplice to keep you under lock and key."

"No," I said, "I'll handle this alone!"

"Or have an accident—fall down a hole . . ."

"Thanks!"

"Or get wrecked at sea and picked up by a ship that hadn't any wireless and was just setting off on a long voyage."

"You're having a wonderful time, aren't you?"

"Well, couldn't you?"

"All ships have radio these days. Besides, what would I get wrecked in?"

"You'd have to buy a boat. You'd like that."

"Oh, sure! I'd sell my château and my two Rolls-Bentleys to pay for it."

"Couldn't you borrow one?"

"Now that you mention it, I probably could, but I still wouldn't fancy getting wrecked. I've been a survivor twice already. And suppose I wasn't picked up?"

"You'd have made the supreme sacrifice, my love. I'd always treasure your memory."

"You wouldn't have much fun going to bed with a memory."

"Now you're being horrid—I'm only trying to help. This boat you say you could borrow—couldn't you get stranded in it somewhere?"

"Only too easily, from what I've heard about it."

She gave a melodramatic sigh. "The trouble is, you haven't sufficient incentive. I make things too easy for you."

"*You* do!—I like that. The woman who won't even pretend she's going to stay overnight with an old school friend because she might get found out!" I drew one of the curtains, cautiously, and peered out. "Heavens!—it's nearly daylight."

"Poor darling!—you'll be dead tomorrow."

"That's all right," I said. "Where I work, no one'll notice."

Chapter Three

If I hadn't been utterly bored with my sedentary, unexciting work on the project and continuously disturbed by my unsatisfied need for Isobel, I don't suppose I'd have given that lunatic conversation another thought. Isobel had thrown her suggestion out as a joke, and that was the obvious way to take it. But as the days dragged on, with no hope of our being able to get together again, the unlikely seed began to germinate. In conference, my thoughts would wander away from the interminable argument to contemplate with interest and pleasure the notion of a stimulating personal adventure. At night, when frustrating mental images of Isobel often kept me from sleep, my mind would constantly revert to what she'd said. Going over the difficulties one by one and trying to think of a way round them was as good a way of passing the time as any—and gradually, without any conscious effort on my part, the dim outline of a plan began to take shape. It had some big gaps in it, and I couldn't take it very seriously—in fact, I'd have said at first that the whole thing was outrageously impracticable. But I was sufficiently intrigued to make some inquiries on a few points, and afterwards it didn't seem impracticable—it merely seemed extremely difficult, which was quite another matter.

However, I didn't think it very likely I'd ever get much further with it. I certainly had no intention, when I next went to the Cowleys, of saying anything to Isobel about it—indeed, I didn't expect to have the opportunity. It was Walter who'd suggested I should drop in for a drink, and naturally I thought he'd be around. But when I showed up just after six thirty, Isobel told me he'd called from the works to say he'd be a little late. So she got some drinks and we sat down very decorously in the drawing room to wait for him.

"Well, how's the plan going?" she asked brightly, as she passed me a Martini.

I was considerably taken aback. "What plan?" I said.

"Darling, don't tell me that when I give you a perfectly marvelous idea on a plate you completely iguore it!"

"Oh, *that!*" I said. I sipped my drink. "But it's absurd."

"There's no harm in thinking about it, is there?"

"Well, no, I suppose not. . . ." I hesitated. Now that she'd raised the subject herself, it seemed stupid not to get her reactions. "As a matter of fact," I said, "I *have* been turning it over in my mind. Purely as a mental exercise, of course."

"Oh, of course!"

"It's quite interesting, actually. That idea of yours about getting marooned in a boat—it could have possibilities."

"A grudging acknowledgment," she said, "but do go on—I'm longing to hear all about it. Where would you maroon yourself?"

"Well—it would obviously have to be an island or there'd be no reasonable excuse for staying there. An uninhabited island, too."

She nodded encouragingly. "That sounds simple enough—there are plenty of uninhabited islands scattered around, aren't there?"

"Not plenty it would be possible to reach in a small boat that happens to be stuck away at the moment in an east-coast creek. Precious few, when you start looking into it."

She smiled. "If you're waiting for me to guess, I give up."

"Well," I said, "if I *were* going to attempt the thing, I think I'd go for the Farne Islands."

"The Farne Islands . . . I've heard of them, of course, but that's about all. Where are they?"

"They're two or three miles off the coast of Northumberland, not very far from the Border. To tell you the truth, I didn't know much about them myself until I looked them up."

"You cagey old thing! I believe you've really been quite busy on this."

"Oh, it's only that I like messing about with maps and charts.

... Anyway, the islands are very tiny, some of them just rocks, and there are quite a lot of them. They're uninhabited, they're a bird sanctuary, and they belong to the National Trust. People don't start visiting them much till the early summer, and there are several that aren't visited at all."

"Why, they sound perfect."

I grinned. "They sound bleak to me!"

"Darling, you know you're used to exposure.... How would you get marooned, though?"

"Oh, the boat would break down near the island I'd chosen."

"Really break down?"

"Yes. Genuine accident-on-purpose. No possibility of repair."

"In that case, how could you be certain of getting away when you were ready?"

"If the worst came to the worst," I said, "I could always swim. I'd choose an island that wasn't too far from the mainland—there's one biggish rock not much more than a mile and a half from the shore that might do quite well."

"Can you really swim as far as that?"

"Oh, yes, in a quiet sea."

"You must be pretty good. I'm not bad, either—I love swimming. We must swim together sometime, darling, with nothing on—it's much more fun.... Wait a minute, though. If you could get off in the end by swimming, why couldn't you have done it to start with? How would you be marooned?"

"I thought of that, but there's no real difficulty. When I came to tell my story afterwards, I'd say I hadn't been sure whether I could manage the distance. After all, I'm the only person who could possibly be a judge of that. I'd say I'd been afraid I might drown, so I'd tried everything else and only taken to the water as a last resort."

"What do you mean by 'everything else'?"

"Well, I'd make signals of various kinds—only I'd take care they weren't visible until I was ready to leave."

"Yes, I see.... You're really quite clever, aren't you?"

"The Admiralty think so."

"I'd love them to hear you now ...! And how long would you stay on the island?"

"Oh, I don't know—it would depend a good deal on the weather. Anything up to a fortnight, I suppose."

"Would that be long enough for the papers to say nasty things about you?"

"I dare say a week would be long enough if the false trail was a convincing one. Anyway, I could take a portable radio with me and listen in to see how things were going."

"What time of year would be best?"

"I should think about April. There'd be no one around then—and with luck there might be birds' eggs to eat."

"You don't mean you'd live on birds' eggs for a fortnight?"

"Good heavens, no, I'd take stores with me—but of course I'd pretend afterwards that I'd only had an odd tin or two. The birds' eggs would supplement the diet and give a bit of color to the story."

"It begins to sound quite thrilling, doesn't it? But what would you be doing up in Northumberland in the first place? You'd have to have a good reason."

"I'd have the best of all reasons—I'd have taken the boat up the coast for pleasure. I've always wanted to do a bit of inshore cruising—I don't know why I've never got around to it before."

"You've been too busy with your young women, darling."

I ignored that. "Anyway, that's what I'd do—I'd cruise up the coast and leave the boat tucked away in some quiet spot, perhaps in the Firth of Forth, and then at the right moment I'd collect it and set off for the islands."

"It sounds quite an undertaking—the trip up the coast, I mean."

"It could be—but that would be one of the attractions."

"And what about the false trail?"

"Well, there'd be no trouble about mislaying a few top-secret documents—I've thought of a way of doing that so that it would look suspicious at the time without getting me into hot water afterwards."

"You said before that no one would notice."

"And you said I'd have to make them notice, which was quite

right. I'd have to do something to start them searching. For instance, if I were last seen in some port that a Russian ship had just sailed from—some port where, as far as anyone knew, I had no legitimate business—they'd soon begin wondering if my files were in order."

"What legitimate business could you have?"

"I'd be on my way to pick up my boat. I'd obviously have to have some railhead for getting to it, and that could easily be a port—say Leith, for instance. I haven't checked, but Soviet steamers probably trade in there occasionally. Anyway, there are other places. No one would know about the boat at the time, of course, but it would give me a complete explanation when I needed it."

"Would you be able to find out about the ship's movements beforehand?"

"Yes, if I kept an eye on Lloyd's list. There'd be no difficulty about that."

"You'd have to make quite sure you were remembered at the port, wouldn't you?—otherwise there'd be no trail and the whole thing would be a flop."

"I agree—and that's actually the biggest snag of all. I'd need a damn good reason for drawing attention to myself. I've been toying with your idea of a last-minute message—a telegram sent from the port just before I left would be perfect, especially if it could be worded in such a way as to help the deception. But who would I send it to, and why?"

"What exactly would you want to convey?"

"Well, ideally I'd want to strengthen the impression that a traitor had abandoned his country—but afterwards the message would have to seem quite natural and innocent."

"Heavens, that's a tall order."

"That's why I'm stuck."

"You mean you'd want it to be something vague like—well—'Can't stand it any longer. Decided to make a clean break'?"

"That's exactly the sort of thing—but what innocent reason could I possibly have for sending that sort of message to anyone?"

"It sounds to me like a last despairing cry to an unresponsive girl friend!"

"I haven't got an unresponsive girl friend."

"Perhaps we could arrange that."

"You underrate me."

She gave me a sidelong smile and was silent for a minute or two. Then she said, "I know—suppose you found a girl and made violent love to her and asked her to marry you and she refused. You could put on a broken-hearted act and at the right moment you could have a terrific scene with her and then fling off to Leith or wherever it was and send that telegram."

"Suppose she said she *would* marry me?"

"That would be quite easy to prevent. If she showed any signs of falling for you in a big way—and I really don't underestimate your charms—you'd simply have to become so beastly to her that she couldn't go through with it."

"There's a naughty sparkle in your eye," I said. "I believe you're just a procuress at heart."

"Oh, I wouldn't want to deprive anyone of a little fun, darling—though you'd have to be a bit careful because it would all come out afterwards."

"H'm! I must say your scheme doesn't awfully appeal to me. It's ingenious, of course—it's brilliant!—but the girl might have feelings."

"She'd soon get over that. Besides, if you played your cards properly she wouldn't much like you, so there'd be nothing to get over."

"All the same, you can't just play around with people like that."

"Why not?—it's done all the time. I'm sure you've often done it."

"Not cold-bloodedly."

"What difference does that make? The result's the same."

"You're a callous type, aren't you?"

"And you're a sentimentalist, in spite of your cynical pose. Fond of children and animals, I wouldn't be surprised! Why do tough men always have soft spots?"

I laughed. "Anyway, it would be a frightful job finding the right girl."

"I don't think so. As a matter of fact, I believe I know the very one."

"You would!"

"She's a physiotherapist at the West Central Clinic—she gave me some massage last year. She's about twenty-two."

"What's she like?"

"Oh, very wholesome, darling. Once she got to know you I'm sure she wouldn't approve of you at all. She's attractive, though—fresh complexion, fair curly hair—she wouldn't be any hardship."

"What's her background?"

"I've no idea—but she's got a very nice foreground!"

"You're incorrigible. What's the name of this beauty queen?"

"Lesley Ashe."

"H'm!—pretty name."

"You could at least meet her, darling, and see what you thought—there'd be no harm in that."

I shook my head. "There'd be no point, either. You seem to be forgetting that all this is only a mental exercise."

"*Is* it?" she said.

"But of course—the whole thing's obviously preposterous."

"I don't see why. Clive, we want to go off and live together, don't we?—and this does make it a possibility. At the moment, I can't think of anything else that does."

"We'd never get away with it."

"We might. It's a wonderful plan, and if you do a bit more work on it . . ."

At that moment Walter drove up in a cab, and we had to drop the subject.

Chapter Four

If I thought about our conversation at all during the next week or two, it was only in the most desultory way. For one thing, the weather was abominable—raw and gray and very cold—and my interest in islands and boats and open-air adventure had dropped with the thermometer. Also, I still found the whole scheme quite remote from reality, even in its improved form. I couldn't imagine myself ever bridging the huge gap between theory and action. I certainly couldn't imagine myself seeking out and laboriously getting to know a wholesome girl in whom I had no interest, even if she was presentable. Talking about the plan had become a diverting pastime, but if Isobel and I really wanted more time together we'd have to find a simpler way, and I hadn't lost hope that in the end she'd accept some risk to make it possible.

I didn't see her again until a day or two before Christmas, when she gave a cocktail party for some of Walter's business friends. There are few functions I loathe more unless they're very small and intimate, and I knew I'd feel hopelessly out of place in this particular gathering. But Isobel positively insisted I should look in, if only to "leaven the lump" as she put it, so I hadn't much choice. I got there as late as I decently could, and there were about thirty people in the drawing room all screaming at the tops of their voices and sweating in the close heat. I took a drink from a young woman with a tray and glanced around over the neighboring heads, and almost at once Isobel spotted me and came weaving through the crush in my direction. She had a girl in tow.

"Hullo!" she cried gaily. "I'm so glad you could make it. Lesley, this is Commander Clive Easton. . . . Clive, I want you to meet

Lesley Ashe. She's an absolute sweetie!—and a wonderful masseuse. Look after her, won't you?" She gave me a wicked smile and melted away.

I had to award her full marks for tenacity, but I felt more than a little peeved at the cunning way she'd sprung the encounter on me without warning. Still, there was nothing I could do about it now—and I could see that talking to Lesley wasn't going to be anything like the ordeal I'd supposed. The girl was *most* attractive—rather taller than average and slim in the right places, with honey-colored hair done in short, crisp curls and an open, friendly smile.

I switched on the charm, and we were soon getting on extremely well together. Isobel had evidently told her something about me already and roused her interest, but I didn't want to talk about submarines, and I soon steered the conversation to her own job, which she obviously found absorbing. I asked her if she ever managed to get any time off, and she laughed and said not much but she did have an occasional evening. From there we got onto the subject of shows, and she said she'd heard that *Hither and Thither* was about the most amusing revue in town, and I said I'd like to see it too. I seemed to have reached a dangerous corner with alarming speed—I suppose it must have been force of habit—and as I was far from clear what I intended to do about her I began to consider how I could gracefully detach myself.

But I was reckoning without Isobel. As the crowd started to thin out she caught my eye and said, "Don't rush off, Clive—we've a small supper laid on." I soon realized that she'd made careful plans. A couple of Walter's friends were lingering—an elderly manufacturer, who was down from Coventry, and his wife—and so was Lesley. I couldn't refuse. We settled ourselves among the debris and had some more drinks, and when the rest of the guests had departed Isobel wheeled in a cold buffet on a tea wagon, which was the nearest thing to a domestic chore I ever saw her engaged in. She placed herself next to the Coventry man's wife, with Walter and his pal busily discussing the price of steel on the other side of her, so that I was left with Lesley as we ate and talked. By now I wasn't exactly stone cold sober, and Lesley was prettily flushed and vivacious, and the evening passed most pleasantly.

At ten thirty Lesley said she must go. Isobel said, "Clive will run you home—he's got his car outside." Lesley protested that it wasn't necessary, but Isobel overruled her before I could say a word. We made our adieus—and as we left Isobel murmured in my ear, "No faltering, now!" Lady Macbeth had nothing on Isobel!

I was still debating what I would do as we passed the Albert Memorial on our way to Kensington. Silence now would probably put an end to Isobel's dubious scheme. But I was feeling mellow, and I told myself that merely seeing Lesley again wouldn't commit me one way or the other. As I stopped the car outside the mews flat where she lived I said, "Well, it's been great fun meeting you. I suppose I couldn't persuade you to come and see that revue with me?"

She hesitated, but only for a second. "I'd like to very much," she said.

The theater visit was quite successful. Lesley seemed to find me a satisfactory escort, and I rather enjoyed the novelty of taking out a young girl. I still hadn't any definite intentions about her, but I thought she might help to fill a temporary gap in my life, and the following week I asked her to dine with me again. We had an agreeable if unexciting evening. She was very friendly, she obviously liked me, and she had no objection to being kissed in the taxi—though that was as far as we got. We parted without making any speciflc arrangement to meet again, chiefly because she was going to be busy. There was, I now realized, no danger of my getting entangled with her very quickly, because she was one of the world's workers and had private patients several evenings a week as well as having to put in regular hours at the clinic. The situation suited me admirably. She was an intelligent, sensitive girl, besides being a charming landscape, but I wouldn't have wanted to have her around very often. Her companionship would, I felt sure, have been a constant delight to anyone who was really interested in her, but she didn't stir me at all, and I found her a very inadequate substitute for Isobel She would make somebody a good wife, which Isobel never would, but I missed the sophistication, the sparkle, and the bitchiness. I couldn't see Lesley ever driving a man to distraction.

Our mild affair was no more than under way when, about the middle of January, Walter went off on his trip to Paris, and at last I was able to see Isobel alone again. It had been an intolerably long interval, and we had quite a conflagration at our first meeting. It wasn't until the early hours, when the fires had temporarily burned out and we were ready to talk, that Isobel said, "And how are you getting on with your Ashe blonde, darling?"

"Oh—we're very good friends," I told her.

"Splendid! And when are you going to move on from there?"

"Probably never, I should think."

"Well, if I were you I should think again, because there's some rather bad news. If you don't do something drastic, it looks as though you and I are going to be washed up pretty soon."

"What do you mean?"

"Walter's doctor says he's got to take things more gently and not tear about so much. He's going to make two more trips that he's already arranged and then one of the other directors will be doing most of the traveling. Walter will be staying at home—with me."

I gave a rather sickly grin. Sometimes she was subtle, and sometimes she wasn't, and this was one of the times she wasn't. "You wouldn't be playing hard-to-keep, would you?" I said.

"No, of course not."

"Getting tired of me?"

"Don't be absurd, darling. Do I *act* as though I'm tired?"

"Then it looks to me as though you'll have to take up those evening classes after all."

"*Oh*, no!" she said. "It's up to you."

"You're trying to force my hand," I said, "and I'm not sure I care for it very much."

"Darling, I'm not trying to force your hand at all—I'm just telling you what the position is. I expect we'd be able to go on meeting occasionally in any case, but the thing is it couldn't possibly be often, and I wouldn't like that any more than you would. You know I can't do without you."

"You want me on your terms, though."

"But naturally!"

I considered the position in gloomy silence. Of course, I could tell her to go to hell and hope that she'd give way in the end—but I no longer thought that she would, so where would it get me? In spite of what she'd said, I felt pretty sure I needed her more than she needed me. That was her strength, and she knew it. The time would come, inevitably, when my passion for her would be finally spent—and in an affair so largely physical as ours, it could come quickly. But it hadn't come yet, and that, at the moment, was what counted. The urge to hold onto her had never been stronger.

"Look," I said at last, "you don't *seriously* think we should try to pull this thing off, do you? It's too fantastic."

"It won't seem fantastic when you stop thinking of it as an exercise and get down to hard work."

"But it's full of the most frightful snags."

"You'll enjoy getting over them."

"I wonder . . .! What I particularly don't like is the Lesley aspect. I'm scared of it."

"You'll just have to be brave, darling!"

"I still think she might say 'Yes.' "

"She won't if you don't want her to. All you need to do is get a bit tight, or pretend to, and throw the suggestion at her. She'll have far too much pride to say 'Yes.' At the very worst she'll only say 'Perhaps,' and after that you can easily put her off. The main thing at the moment is to get your proposal on the record."

I shook my head. "It isn't, you know. If we *were* going on with this crazy idea, the main thing would be to check up on the boat. There's absolutely no point in my getting involved with Lesley if the boat's too ramshackle to take me up the coast."

"All right," she said, "then go and look at the boat first. As long as you get on with things, I'm quite happy to leave the actual arrangements to you." She smiled her faintly mocking smile. "After all, you're the Commander!"

I knew very little about the boat, except that she was a small cabin cruiser and her name was *Shelduck*. She belonged to a friend of mine in the Hydrographic Department—a chap named Benson, who had recently gone off to the West Indies on a charting expedition and would be away till the late summer. He'd told me I was welcome to use the cruiser for a spot of fishing or for anything else I fancied, but strictly at my own risk! I knew that she wasn't in very good condition, and that he'd left her unattended in the Walton backwaters because he didn't think she was worth the expense of putting in anyone's charge. She could hardly have sounded less promising, and I felt pretty sure that once I'd seen her I'd have no option but to turn down the plan on grounds of sheer hazard. That at least would save a lot of argument, even if it didn't solve our problems.

I waited for the weather to improve, and one bright, frosty Saturday towards the end of January I got into some old clothes and slung a pair of dilapidated rubber boots and my binoculars into the back of the Ford and drove into Essex with an inch-to-the-mile map of the Walton district in my pocket. I knew the backwaters fairly well, for I'd spent most of an Easter vacation sailing there when I'd been up at Cambridge. They lie just north of Walton-on-the-Naze and just south of Harwich, and consist of a broad tidal inlet with a big island in the center called Horsey Island and lots of creeks and channels going off in all directions. The Naze itself throws a protecting arm around them, keeping out the sea, and a small boat can lie there safely in almost any conditious.

Benson had said his boat was berthed off the Walton channel, which was marked on the map. I took the road towards the Naze, parked the car among some low bushes, and struck off briskly for the sea wall. The tide was out, and the creek was no more than a thin trickle of water with banks of gray-brown mud sloping up to saltings on either side. There were several small boats snugged down for the winter in little rills, but I could see no sign of any of their owners, which was just as well. I studied each of them in turn through my glasses, and presently I picked out a small cruiser that had to be *Shelduck*. She was drawn well up on the saltings and would need a fair tide to float her. After another hundred yards or so I could make out her name.

At first sight, she looked a wretched old "tore-out." The winter storms had stripped her of whatever varnish she'd once had, the black paint on her hull was peeling, and by the smell of her she was pretty rotten. She was about twenty feet long, with a two-berth cabin and a small galley near the door on the starboard side and an open cockpit housing an engine under a wooden cover. I took the cover off, and I thought the engine looked in better shape than the rest of the boat. It was a four-cylinder marine job, and from its size I imagined it would give *Shelduck* a good turn of speed if I ever got it going. I found the key to the cabin in the stem locker where Benson had left it, had a look round inside, and saw there was a little basic equipment, but not much. On the cabin top, temporarily stowed, was a very small, very decrepit dinghy and a couple of battered oars. I poked around for some time, examining the anchor and chain and the rudder fastenings and sticking a knife blade into the more doubtful-looking planks. She was certainly a bit soft, but I'd seen worse.

I'd intended to return to London that afternoon, but my interest was aroused, and instead I drove into Walton and looked up the tide tables for the next day in an almanac in the public library. The odds were heavily against a tide that would get *Shelduck* off the saltings, but when I glanced down the column I saw that by sheer chance I'd hit on a week end of extremely big ones. The opportunity to give the boat a trial run and perhaps move her to a more convenient berth if she behaved satisfactorily seemed too good to miss. I booked a room at a hotel in Walton, and that evening I got out my map and carefully studied the various approaches to the creeks. I soon found what I wanted. There was a place deep inside the back-waters where an old cart track from a minor road came to an end just under the sea wall. It was well away from the main small-boat anchorage, and yet it was accessible from the land by car, which would be important if I ever got as far as loading gear and provisions aboard. Also, it was a place where *Shelduck* would float at every tide, which meant I'd have no difficulty in getting away at short notice if the occasion arose.

I was out early next morning. I drove along the London road until I found a garage that was open, and bought a can of petrol and some oil and a set of spark plugs. Then I returned quickly to the backwaters. I reached *Shelduck* around ten, just as the saltings were beginning to cover, and climbed aboard her. She started to make a little water as the tide rose, but it was less than I expected considering she'd been drying out there all winter, and I knew the planks would soon take up. I checked the engine oil and changed the plugs, and to my surprise the engine started at the third swing, with a nice healthy note. Even the water pump worked.

By now the weather had become dull and very chilly, and although it was Sunday morning I had the creeks and saltings to myself again. I lost no time in getting off. Directly *Shelduck* swung on her chain I got the anchor and took her out into the channel and steered northward down Walton Creek on full throttle. If anything, she was overengined, and I reckoned her speed to be nearly ten knots in still water. Provided she didn't shake all her calking out, she'd be capable of covering a lot of sea. In almost no time at all I'd rounded the northern tip of Horsey Island, and by slack water I was cautiously feeling my way into the new berth. I made the boat secure in a muddy channel just under the sea wall, and as soon as she'd taken the ground I scrambled ashore and set off back to the car by road.

It had been an exhilarating morning, and my mood was transformed. *Shelduck*, I now saw, had as good a chance of making the passage up the coast in the right weather as any boat of her type. The first stage of the plan was not only feasible—it was definitely attractive, the sort of thing I could embark upon with zest. The other problems could be coped with—even the problem of Lesley! I still found it hard to believe that Isobel's dream of an easy fortune would ever materialize, but whether it did or not I couldn't see that I stood to lose anything. If at some point I ran into insuperable difficulties—if I failed to reach the Forth, or the islands proved unsuitable for my purpose, or the newspapers didn't take the line they were intended to, or the final gamble appeared to be insufficiently lucrative to make it worth while—well, there'd still be time to draw back. I'd have done nothing unlawful until the moment when I actually put in a claim for damages, and I needn't make up my mind about that until right at the end. At least I'd have satisfied my pent-up longing for action and excitement, and broken the deadly monotony of the office routine. It was an inspiriting thought. One way and another, the temptation to have a crack at the thing had suddenly become irresistible.

Chapter Five

It was clear that I couldn't think of mentioning marriage to Lesley without some further preparation of the ground, for we were still scarcely more than friendly acquaintances, and any sudden expression of deep feeling on my part would have sounded wholly unconvincing. From now on, therefore, I started to cultivate her assiduously. I began by telephoning her and saying it seemed ages since I'd seen her and couldn't we meet again? Having set the ball rolling, I kept it on the move. On one pretext or another, I was soon ringing her up almost every evening. My manner became less frivolous than it had been in the past. I began to take a more continuous interest in her work, to ask about her friends, to show more curiosity about her background. I claimed more and more of her free time. The fact that she had so little made it possible for me to appear pressing without having to shoulder any undue burden. Still, we got around quite a bit. Once, on a day of pale winter sunshine, we drove out into Sussex and walked over the Downs. Twice I took her to a cinema, and twice she asked me along for coffee at her flat. The intervals were nicely spaced. About the middle of February she had her twenty-third birthday, and I sent her a bouquet of red roses. Isobel thought the choice unoriginal but congratulated me in principle.

All the time, I tried to keep my finger on her emotional pulse. Its beat, I thought, was vigorous rather than violent. She was undoubtedly attracted to me and flattered by my attentiveness, and I felt sure the idea must have crossed her mind by now that I might someday offer myself as a possible husband, but if the prospect excited her she didn't show it. She was, I decided, a very level-headed young woman, with a strong sense of independence and dignity. What she noticeably did do, as the days went by, was to try to probe more deeply into my own thoughts and feelings—which was sensible of her if she wanted to make up her mind about me, though in fact it couldn't have helped her much. The way I presented myself to her, I must have seemed quite unfathomable. When she was thoughtful and serious and obviously anxious to find some solid basis for our friendship, I flirted with her and teased her and made cautious love to her by glance and gesture and fired off empty gallantries. When she showed any sign of romantic impulses, I became cynical and blasé and bitter about Life! She must often have wondered what the hell was happening to her, and I'm sure she felt hurt and humiliated when she found she couldn't rely on a consistent attitude two days running. Sometimes she became quite distant herself, and then of course I was as nice as could be. I often felt sickened by the part I was playing, but I took comfort from the fact that the climax of our affair was now very near.

I had a little trouble making the all-important date, because Lesley had a sudden rush of patients—or else she was deliberately being difficult. However, it was arranged in the end. I'd decided that a restaurant would provide the most favorable setting, because I'd have better opportunities for steady drinking, and in semipublic it would be easier for me to put my proposal in an offhand way. I chose a cozy little spot in Soho, and Lesley met me there just before eight. I knocked back a couple of Martinis while she toyed with a glass of sherry, and I drank the greater part of a bottle of claret over the meal. I also did most of the talking. I started to reminisce about the war and to describe some of my exploits in a boastful way. I referred unfeelingly to the survivors of some supply junks that the H95 had sunk in the Pacific. I recalled my meeting with Walter Cowley and said some spiteful things about him. I also complained about my job and implied that I was a brilliant fellow who was wasting his talents.

Lesley listened with a baffled expression on her face. These were new facets of my character, and I could see that she was far from attracted by them. Indeed, she grew so restive that I was afraid she might suggest leaving, and I hurriedly switched the conversation to more pleasant topics. My pitch, I felt sure, was already sufficiently queered! At last, when the place had almost emptied and we were quiet in our corner, I took a deep breath and leaned across the table, almost knocking over my second glass of brandy, and said, "Lesley, why don't we get married?"

I thought she turned rather pale, but it could have been some trick of the light. For a while she didn't answer. Then she said quietly, "I don't think that would be a very good idea."

"Why not?"

"Well, for one thing I don't think you're in love with me."

"But I am, darling, desperately. I have been ever since I first saw you."

She looked at me for a long time. There was a wistful air about her, as though a prospect of happiness had somehow faded and she couldn't understand why.

"Well," she said, "I'm afraid I'm not in love with you."

"Not a bit?"

"I don't think so."

"We've got on very well together."

"Sometimes we have. . . . But I don't think it would work."

This was so nearly a refusal that I decided I could afford to put on the pressure. "How do you know?" I demanded.

She hesitated. "Well, there's rather a big difference in our ages, for one thing, and you're so much more experienced than I am, and . . ." She broke off. "No, it isn't that, really—it's just that I can't see myself married to you. It feels all wrong. I don't know why, but it does. . . . I can't feel you're really serious."

"But I am," I said earnestly. "I've never wanted anything so much in my life. If you say 'No' I don't know what I'll do. . . . Won't you think about it, at least?"

"I won't be able to help thinking about it," she said, "but I'm sure it wouldn't be a good idea. I like being with you, but . . . Can't we just go on as we are, being friends?"

I gave a moody shrug. "I don't know that that's going to be very easy now," I said. "I've probably ruined everything by speaking out, but it's difficult just to be friends with a girl when you've told her you love her. . . . And I never did care for half measures."

"I don't think you know what you want," she said.

"You're the strangest person."

By now the waiter was hovering with the bill—I'd timed things well—and soon afterwards we left. I felt immensely relieved. Lesley's feelings were not, after all, deeply involved. I'd cleared the worst hurdle with a good deal less difficulty than I'd expected. No doubt my proposal had seemed abrupt and lacking in warmth, and my attempts at persuasion afterwards had been jejune and cliché-ridden; but on the whole I felt I'd done quite a workman-like job. The necessary words had been spoken and the proposal rejected, and that was all that mattered. From now on, I told myself, I'd be back in my depth again.

I took her home in a taxi as usual. She was very quiet in her corner, and I didn't feel much like talking myself. I was thankful when we finally turned into the mews. I leaned across and gave her a good-night kiss in the routine way, and she seemed to accept it passively. Then, quite suddenly, she threw her arms round my neck and kissed me as she had never done before, and bolted out of the cab. A second later I heard her door slam.

For a moment I sat there transfixed. My face was damp, and I realized she must have been crying. After her composure in the restaurant I couldn't understand it. I began to have a horrible feeling that I'd completely misread her.

Chapter Six

I felt sorry about Lesley for a day or two, but I didn't allow the thought of her to prey on my mind. I was already looking ahead. As soon as I could, I rang Isobel and told her what had happened. She seemed very pleased with the way things had gone. She assured me that a slight emotional storm was only natural after a young girl had been proposed to for the first time, and said that anyway you couldn't make omelets without breaking eggs—a phrase I hadn't heard since the bloodier days of the war. She was obviously prepared for any sacrifice as long as it was made by someone else. However, that was no new discovery, and her very candor somehow disarmed criticism.

The fact that I wasn't seeing Lesley made it much easier not to worry about her. My line was that I preferred for the moment to nurse my disappointment alone, and though I telephoned her once or twice, just to keep things simmering, I avoided committing myself to a meeting. That left me free to get on with the next item on the agenda, which was the preparation of *Shelduck* for her trip to the north.

Chiefly, it was a question of laying in stores and equipment—a job that needed care. I had to think not only of the passage up the coast but also of the final stages of the plan, and that meant there were things I must omit from the inventory as well as things I must remember. I had to be suitably handicapped when I reached the island, and the presence of a saw or an ax aboard might prove almost as great an embarrassment as a box of signal rockets. I could always drop unwanted articles in the sea, of course, but if it ever emerged—as it well might—that I had bought useful tools and gear that I had inexplicably lost, there might be awkward questions. I much preferred to have everything worked out beforehand to the last detail. Adventure, someone had said, was the failure of organization; and though I couldn't entirely agree, I took the point well enough. Slow, methodical planning followed by quick, decisive execution was the only way to ensure a successful campaign.

The shopping expedition itself raised an immediate problem. I didn't want any ship's chandler suddenly remembering, when my picture came to be published in the papers after my disappearance, that I was a man he'd supplied with a lot of boat stuff. An absolutely vital part of the whole plan was that no one should associate me with a boat at all until I reappeared and told them about it. I decided that a modest disguise was the answer—though one that wouldn't strike anyone as having been a disguise when the facts came out. On a raw Saturday morning, therefore, I pulled a woolen scarf well round my chin and a cloth cap well down over my forehead and stuck a strip of plaster over one cheekbone as though I'd cut myself shaving. Having satisfied myself that I looked different but not peculiar, I took the car round to a busy little chandler's shop near the Minories. I picked out the things I wanted, quickly and without fuss, paid cash for them, and took them away. There was a fair amount of gear, from a new kedge anchor to prickers for the paraffin stove, but it all went comfortably into the capacious trunk of the car. I also bought some special clothing at the same shop—a duffel coat, a jersey, a beret, and a new pair of rubber boots—which would stay locked up in the trunk with the rest of the stuff. These were the clothes I proposed to wear at the time of my disappearance, so it was important that no one should know I had them. It would upset everything if the police, in the course of their inevitable inquiries, learned that I had had such an outfit and that it was missing.

By the end of the third week in February I had everything ready for loading. Locked away in my garage were several cans of petrol that I'd picked up at places where I wasn't known; a large box of provisions, mostly canned, that I'd bought in small quantities at different shops; and a big water container that I'd filled at the garage tap. I'd also equipped myself with fishing tackle and a new cheap portable radio. I already had one in the flat, but I'd want to leave that for the police to find. I could always say afterwards that it had been too good a model to take on a boat, if anyone wondered why I'd bought another.

That Saturday morning, having checked up on the tides, I took the whole carload down to *Shelduck*. The day was vile, with almost continuous rain, but it suited me well, for it meant there was no risk of anyone seeing me at work. As far as I could judge, no one had been near the place in my absence—the only marks in the mud between the shore and the boat were the ones I had made myself. The moving of *Shelduck* to her new berth had evidently aroused no active curiosity in the district.

I got wet and filthy humping all the stuff over the sea wall and across the mud, but I managed to put the whole lot aboard in a grueling couple of hours. I did a few essential jobs around the ship in what was left of the daylight, and by dusk she was as ready for passage-making as she was ever likely to be. She'd have won no prizes in a *concours d'élégance*, but I thought she'd do the job. I drove back to town that night exhausted but satisfied.

My main anxiety now was the weather. At present there were rain and wind every day, and in such conditions I couldn't hope to put to sea. I got out maps and charts and did some simple calculations, and I made it the best part of four hundred miles by water from Walton to Leith. Allowing for contrary tides, I couldn't count on doing much more than eighty miles a day even in the most favorable circumstances, which meant that I'd be wise to reckon on at least a week for the trip. I had some leave owing to me, and I didn't think there'd be any difficulty about getting away—but choosing a week of tolerable weather was another matter. If the spring turned out to be anything like the recent average, I might still be crawling up the coast by midsummer!

However, there was no immediate urgency, and I still had things to do. I spent several absorbing evenings working out in great detail alternative stages for my passage up the coast and familiarizing myself as far as possible with the buoys and channels and harbor approaches and the likeliest places for refueling. I also began to prepare the way at the office by having a private talk with George Grey, my chief. Grey was a rather distinguished-looking man in his late fifties, with a balding, well-shaped head and keen blue eyes. He was an urbane and civilized type, with a long family tradition of public service; and he took pride in having loyal and happy colleagues around him. That made it easy. Over a drink I mentioned that I was feeling a bit depressed over some personal trouble, and I told him enough about Lesley to interest without embarrassing him. He didn't seem altogether surprised—in fact he said it had struck him lately that I'd been looking as though I had something on my mind! He was very sympathetic, and himself suggested that a change might do me good. I said perhaps I'd go off and do a bit of fishing when the weather improved, and he thought that an excellent idea.

However, the weather didn't improve. As one blustery day succeeded another, I began to wonder whether the sea trip ever would be practicable. I even started to consider alternative arrangements. It would be possible, I knew, to get a contractor to collect *Shelduck* from Walton and take her north overland and dump her at a convenient spot near Leith. It might strike someone afterwards as a rather surprising operation for a casual yachtsman, but if I explained that I'd been very keen to explore those waters I could probably get away with it. I'd have been happier, though, if she'd been my own boat—moving someone else's four hundred miles by road was bound to seem a bit of a liberty. Sailing up the coast and happening to get that far was quite another matter. There were other difficulties, too. The real trouble, apart from the considerable expense, was that at some point I'd probably have to discuss the job with the contractor in person, and he'd be practically certain to remember me when the hue and cry started. Still, there might be some way round that, and I continued to toy with the notion.

Then, right at the end of the month, the weather changed. The barometer started a slow, steady rise as a high-pressure system moved in from Scandinavia, and March came in like a lamb, with a perfect spring day. What was more important, it promised to remain a lamb for the best part of a week. My luck was in. I quickly fixed up ten days' leave, rang up Isobel and told her I was off, and on the second day of the month traveled by train to Walton and went aboard *Shelduck*. I moved her at high water, anchored for the night just inside the Walton channel, and sailed at crack of dawn on the first of the ebb. Conditions were absolutely perfect. There was the gentlest of zephyrs, the surface of the sea was scarcely rippled, and the barometer was as steady as a rock. I felt in terrific spirits.

During the next few days I had a wonderful holiday, and for long periods I almost forgot the purpose of my journey in the pleasure of being at sea again. The sun was amazingly warm, and I had little to do but bask in it. Visibility was good all the time, and as long as I kept close inshore and watched the buoys and landmarks and kept the engine running I couldn't go wrong. The merest tyro could have made the trip. For hours at a time I left the tiller lashed and let the little ship motor northwards on her own. The dinghy, on tow, slowed me a bit, but I did my eighty miles a day easily. With no sudden emergencies to face, planning my overnight stops was child's play. Whenever I could, I put into one of the east-coast rivers and anchored there in some quiet spot. If there wasn't a river, there was always a small harbor. It was cold at night, but I had a Service sleeping bag and the cabin was snug. I refueled several times, taking the empty cans ashore in the dinghy and carrying them to near-by garages. I talked to people as little as possible, and I particularly avoided other yachtsmen, who would have been certain to show interest in my trip. Not that I was much concerned now about being remembered—with my deep tan, my growth of beard, my old clothes and my beret, I didn't look in the least like the higher civil servant whose photograph might one day appear in every newspaper. But it seemed better to take no risks.

It wasn't until the morning of the fifth day that the weather began to cause me any concern. I'd spent the night at anchor in the Tyne, and at first light I set off once more up the coast on what should have been the last leg but one of the trip. But the glass was slowly falling, and the early forecast hadn't been good. By three o'clock the wind had backed and strengthened, the sky had clouded over, and the sea was beginning to get up. I was just about abreast of the Farnes then, and I couldn't miss the chance to take a look at the island I'd provisionally chosen as my ultimate objective. It was an isolated rock called the Megstone, and I soon picked it out. I steered close and made a circuit of it, examining its approaches with care. It was a grim and inhospitable place, but it promised to be ideal for what I had in mind. I'd have liked to go ashore and inspect it more thoroughly, but by now there was too much surf for a landing, and in any case I didn't dare to linger. *Shelduck*, with her small draught and high; built-up cabin, was already rolling badly, and I knew she'd be a lamentable boat in a real seaway. What I needed now was a safe harbor. I took a quick glance at the chart and another at the sky, and decided to make for Budle Bay, a shallow, sheltered inlet just north of Bamburgh.

In the kind of weather I'd had so far, it would have been no more than twenty minutes' steaming away, but as things were it took me twice that time. There was some very rough going at the entrance to the bay, with a short, steep sea that threw *Shelduck* all over the place, and I had an anxious moment or two when I saw that her whole superstructure was working and threatening to come adrift. But I got through in the end and dropped anchor thankfully in a quiet creek called Waren Burn not far from Budle village. The place was not unlike the Walton backwaters—it had the same expanses of mud, the same gray-green saltings, and the same deserted air. As the tide fell I maneuvered the boat into a good berth; and she took the ground nicely.

I say the bay was sheltered, but I had a noisy night all the same. The wind blew hard, with driving rain, and I slept very little. By morning it was obvious that the weather had finally broken and that I hadn't the slightest chance of getting up to the Firth of Forth. It was exasperating to have come so near to my goal and yet not to have reached it, but it would have been folly to tempt my luck. I had breakfast, tidied myself up a bit, and changed into my shore clothes. The boat clothes would only get damp if I left them, so I packed them away in my bag. I made a rough note of what provisions I still had aboard, and checked the water, petrol, and paraffin. Then I made *Shelduck* secure to two anchors, locked her up, walked about three miles to the nearest station—a small place called Belford—and after a tedious wait and a slow journey on a local train I caught an express to London.

Back at the office, I naturally had to answer a few friendly questions about how I'd spent my leave, but I managed to get by without mentioning the boat and yet without saying anything that might later be regarded as duplicity. I told George Grey that I'd been up to Northumberland and done a bit of sea fishing, which seemed to cover the facts adequately. If later it should be thought that I had been strangely unforthcoming, I could always blame my temporarily morose state. Grey himself, being no fisherman, didn't press me for details. His main concern was to know whether the change had done me good—and on that, with an eye to the future, I was only moderately reassuring.

Chapter Seven

Having got *Shelduck* so far up the coast, I felt that I could go ahead confidently with the next part of the plan. It was true that I would need one long week end of fine weather to complete the trip to the Forth, but with ordinary luck I would get that. Meanwhile, there was a vitally important and extremely tricky stage ahead. I had to build myself up, in rather a short time, as the sort of chap who might take his country's secrets abroad.

The office was the place that mattered most, and from now on I worked hard at putting over a deteriorating personality. I became increasingly moody and short-tempered, and spent long periods at my desk visibly brooding. When, after a week or so, Grey referred again to my state of health, I told him I wasn't sleeping well and that I was thinking of getting my doctor to give me a complete overhaul. In the local pub, where I usually went for a sandwich lunch, I switched my drinking from beer to whiskey and tried to give the impression that I was hitting the bottle hard when any of my colleagues were around. I became much more outspoken about the futility of the project than I'd have considered tactful in ordinary circumstances, and grumbled openly about the conditions of cloistered secrecy in which we worked. In fact, from the way I carried on through March, I was clearly shaping for either prolonged sick leave or an early transfer to some less responsible job. The danger was that I might overdo the act and precipitate a crisis too soon, and I had to be careful about that.

Something still had to be done to suggest a political angle as an alternative to the personal one, which was—and would remain—my own explanation of my behavior. The least hint of ideological unorthodoxy in the office, however, would have finished me at once. I decided that it would be sufficient if I planted a few seeds with Lesley, and one evening I rang her up and said I'd like to see her again. She invited me round to her flat with such readiness that I wondered uneasily if she'd been having second thoughts about my proposal. If she had, they couldn't long have survived my treatment of her. From the moment I saw her, I did nine-tenths of the talking. I said in a sulky tone that I supposed she hadn't changed her mind about me and continued to assume that she hadn't without giving her a chance to say anything. I moaned about my health and my depressed frame of mind in a manner calculated to douse the last spark of romance in any young woman. I went on to denounce my job and my colleagues and the wretched state of the world, and having thoroughly worked myself up I switched splenetically to international politics and the risk of war. I said, in an unprecedented monologue, that we were crazy to have got tied up with America over the Far East and that I didn't believe either Russia or China really intended to start any trouble. I drank two cups of coffee, and said belatedly that I was sorry if I'd seemed boorish, but that it was really her fault, and left her looking pale and worried and completely at a loss. It had been a grim evening for both of us.

Politics didn't mean a thing to Lesley, but I thought my remarks would register with her if only because they were so unusual coming from me—and I knew that when the time came the security boys would prize it all out of her. Just to be on the safe side, though; I said rather similar things to Walter and to one or two other people whom I knew socially. By the end of March I had spread the impression fairly widely that the fine young war hero had become a peevish neurotic whose love affairs had gone wrong, who despised his job, and whose ideas were now running in very dubious political channels. Something had to happen pretty soon, and I watched the weather anxiously.

The last days of March were wild, with gale-force winds, but by the first Friday in April the outlook had improved sufficiently for me to contemplate finishing the trip to the Forth. I decided to travel north that evening, and arranged without difficulty to take a long week end. Then something happened that transformed my plans. I'd recently got into the habit of keeping an eye on the shipping movements so that I could get some idea of the frequency with which Polish and Russian ships were trading into the Forth. That Friday morning I was glancing down Lloyd's list when an item jolted me. A Polish steamer, the *Jan Sobolski*, homeward bound for Gdynia, had put into Berwick-on-Tweed to land a couple of men who'd been injured in an engine-room accident and to make some minor repairs. She was expected to sail again in twenty-four hours.

I realized the possibilities on the instant. I myself had been making for the Tweed when bad weather had forced me into Budle Bay, and Berwick was only twenty miles or so from where I'd left *Shelduck*. Considering how poor the local train service was, I'd have every excuse for using Berwick as my railhead. I felt that Fate had played into my hands. This, undoubtedly, was D-day!

Once I'd made the decision, I lost no time in putting my plans into operation. First I rang Lesley at the clinic and told her I'd got to see her urgently. She was busy, but she said if it was really vital she could get away at twelve. I met her in a pub at Knightsbridge. I said that seeing her again had made me realize I'd simply got to make one more effort. I told her I was absolutely crazy about her, implored her to reconsider her decision, and said I'd got to have her final answer right away. I said that hoping against hope was getting me down and that I couldn't stand it a moment longer. I was feeling pretty excited on other counts, and it wasn't difficult to behave as though I was slightly off my chump. She looked bewildered and a little scared, and when I pressed her with more vehemence than I had any right to show, she naturally said "No." She said it gently, as though she were talking to a refractory patient, but quite firmly. She said again that it would be much better if I could reconcile myself to our being just friends. That was all I needed. I jumped to my feet and left her without another word. Everything had gone perfectly.

I rang Isobel and told her what had happened, and that I was going into action that day. She was very thrilled. I said that all my arrangements were at concert pitch, and that I should be taking food and water for a fortnight and she could expect to hear of my reappearance soon after the middle of April. I told her to keep cool and watch her step. She said she always watched her step, and wished me luck.

Back in the office, I had no difficulty in playing the part of a man who had just made a tremendous decision and was working under strain. That was how I felt; and the odd glances I got from my secretary, Miss Groves, showed that she'd noticed it. I gave her a memorandum to type, to keep her out of the way, and while she was clattering away in her own room I took some of the "classified" documents out of the safe and slipped a couple of the more important top-secret papers into a file of harmless stuff that I'd borrowed from "J" department some days before. Then I rang for a messenger and sent the "J" file back and locked up the "classifieds" in the safe again.

I got away, thankfully, at five thirty. I took a cab to King's Cross and reserved a sleeper on the 12:55 a.m. train to Berwick. Then I went to my flat to make final preparations. I changed from my office clothes into brown tweeds, a light overcoat, and a soft hat, packed my bag with the few things I'd have needed if I'd merely been going north for a week end, and in the garage added the boots, duffel coat, jersey, and beret that had been locked up in the car trunk ever since my return from Budle. I took another cab back to King's Cross and dumped the bag in the cloakroom. I spent the rest of the evening at a quiet little restaurant and at a cinema. I didn't want to risk running into anyone I knew at this stage. I passed the last hour or so in the station waiting room with my hat over my face, apparently dozing, and when the time came to board the train I moved briskly to my sleeper.

I traveled to Berwick in comfort, arriving just after eight in the morning. It was a cool spring day, exhilarating and pleasant. There was an onshore breeze from the north-east, but it was so light that I didn't think it would give me much trouble. I breakfasted at a hotel near the station and then, still wearing my tweeds and looking very respectable, I carried my bag to the bus terminal. There would be a bus at a quarter to twelve, I found, that would take me within easy walking distance of *Shelduck*. I left the bag and set off across a picturesque stone bridge to the harbor, anxious to make sure that the *Jan Sobolski* was still there. If she'd already sailed, the whole enterprise would have to be postponed. But she was there all right, a steamer of a thousand tons or so, tied up in the dock behind locked gates astern of a Finnish timber ship. From the look of her she was pretty well ready to leave, and I guessed she was only waiting for the afternoon tide. As I walked by her I had a moment's concern lest the dock should be one of those one couldn't easily get into, but I needn't have worried. Although it was fenced in, with notices by the harbor commissioners telling unauthorized persons to keep out, the fence was dilapidated and breached at half a dozen points, and I felt sure that with care and the connivance of the crew I could have got aboard the ship unchallenged.

I sauntered up and down for a few minutes before leaving. If anyone afterwards remembered seeing me, it would give additional support to the theory I was trying to put over. At the same time, what could be more understandable than that a sailing man, with an hour or two on his hands before joining his own boat, should wander along to the local harbor to see what was going on there?

Presently I returned across the bridge and found the post office and sent off the all-important telegram to Lesley. I'd given a good deal of thought to the wording, but I'd failed to improve on Isobel's original version—CANT STAND ANY MORE DECIDED TO MAKE CLEAN BREAK GOOD-BY CLIVE. That would be my considered answer to Lesley's offer of friendship without marriage—a formal severing of all ties, an indication that I didn't intend to see her again. If others chose to put a more sinister interpretation on it, the misfortune would be theirs. The girl clerk gave me one quick glance after she'd counted the words, but she didn't say anything. I paid, and left.

At twelve fifteen I went back to the bus station and collected my bag and took it into a near-by public lavatory. When I emerged the tweeds and overcoat and soft hat were in the bag, and I was wearing old flannels, rubber boots, and duffel coat, with my black beret set on my head at a rakish angle. I could easily account for the change of clothing, if I ever had to, on the ground that the boat was out in the mud and that no sensible man would have thought of approaching her in a decent outfit. I looked, perhaps, a little odd even for a yachtsman, but I certainly didn't look like the chap who had got off the night train or sent the telegram, and that was all that mattered.

By now the bus was waiting, and I climbed in and buried my face in a newspaper. When the moment came to buy my ticket I did it absently, avoiding the "clippie's" gaze. The journey passed without incident, and three quarters of an hour later I was on my own again, approaching Budle Bay on foot. *Shelduck* was just as I'd left her, except that she'd swung round a little in her channel. The tide had not yet reached her, and I got aboard without trouble, unpacked my bag, and made everything shipshape. I checked over the stores again and stowed away the few extra things that I'd brought with me. There was still almost a full can of water, not so fresh but drinkable, and about the right amount of petrol in the tank for a week end among the islands, if I'd been going for a week end. I untied the dinghy and made it fast to an old post—I obviously couldn't take it with me or I shouldn't be able to maroon myself. If anyone wondered why I'd left it behind, I should have to explain what a nuisance it had been on tow, and say that I'd preferred not to encumber myself for this short trip. Any sailing man would understand my feeling, even though he might question my wisdom. Finally, I heaved up the two anchors and cleaned them and put them aboard. By now the channel was filling rapidly. The moment *Shelduck* floated I started the engine and got under way. I grounded twice in the winding channel, but after a little maneuvering I found deeper water, and in less than ten minutes I was out of the bay.

It was only a mile or two to the islands and the flood tide wouldn't reach its peak for nearly an hour, so there was no hurry. I set the throttle at half speed and let *Shelduck* make her own way towards the Megstone while I carefully examined the larger islands and the mainland shore and the sea horizon through my glasses. As far as I could judge, there was no one around to take any interest in my movements. No coastwise shipping was bearing down on me. With reasonable luck I would reach my destination unobserved. I put on speed and soon had the rock between myself and the shore. I closed in quickly to its seaward flank until I was cut off from sight of the land. I felt happier, then.

The face of the island was mostly steep-to, but during my earlier inspection I'd noticed that there was one place where the approach was by a succession of rough ledges, and I was relying on this to make a stranding possible. All the same, I could see it was going to be difficult enough. There was an awkward swell and, because I was on the windward side, a good deal of surf. I waited almost until high water, to cut the danger period to a minimum, and then worked the boat in very cautiously towards the ledge until her keel touched.

The next few minutes were distinctly unpleasant. Slight though the sea was compared with what it might have been, the grinding noises that came from *Shelduck's* hull as she was repeatedly swept against the rock set my teeth on edge. Every time a wave receded, she hit the ground with a splintering crash. Water began to pour in through a dozen opened seams, and I feared she might fill and roll over and founder before I could secure her. But the danger passed. Little by little she was driven in over the ledge by the wind and the surf, until presently I was able to leap ashore and get a rope round a projection of rock and hold her until the water level fell. The grinding was now no more than a grumble, and soon she had settled down at a not too uncomfortable angle, high and reasonably dry on a boulder-strewn slope.

For the moment, I was well content. I had pulled off a hazardous feat, even if it could hardly be called a feat of seamanship. I might, of course, have much more trouble with the boat during the next few tides if the weather turned nasty, but at present the barometer was steady. And in a day or two, I knew, that anxiety would pass, for the spring tides were near their peak and once they began to take off she wouldn't float even at high water. For a fortnight or so, she'd be as much a fixture on the island as the rock itself.

Now I had to justify the stranding, and I got to work at once on the petrol pipe. A few turns with a spanner loosened the union nut under the tank, and I sat and watched the petrol drain away into the bilge. The boat would smell foul long after the stuff had evaporated, but that was something I'd have to put up with. As soon as the tank was empty, I attacked the pipe again with a heavier spanner. Only a little force was necessary to break away the old solder where the pipe joined the tank and leave a gaping hole. I inspected the damage, and it looked all right to me. I wouldn't have any difficulty in explaining it when the time came.

Satisfied, I left the boat and set off to explore.

The Megstone was no Robinson Crusoe's isle. It was bare of all vegetation except for a few patches of dark green moss or lichen and a ruffle of brown seaweed at its base. It was less than a hundred yards in length and scarcely half that distance wide. At its highest point it rose no more than eighteen or twenty feet above the water, but its sides were steep and rugged. The conical peak was white with the droppings of generations of cormorants and guillemots that had nested on it. There were no signs of any nests yet, but there were scores of birds, and they made a fiendish row as their sanctuary was invaded.

I climbed cautiously to the top of the rock and sat down to study my surroundings through the glasses. Between myself and the mainland, just under two miles away, there was nothing but empty sea. It held no terrors for me, but I would certainly need no excuse for not committing myself lightly to a swim, and if in my own good time I could get off in a less uncomfortable way I would do so. Immediately opposite me, dominating the shore line, was the great projecting pile of Bamburgh Castle, with a fine sandy beach on both sides of it backed by low dunes and dotted here and there with deserted summer huts. Apart from Bamburgh village and another small place called Seahouses, whose tiny harbor I could just make out about three miles to the south, the coast was free from buildings and quite unspoiled. Undulating, sheep-grazed fields stretched away inland to the distant Cheviots. I had no cause to complain of the view, however much I might tire of it!

I turned to examine, the other islands. The nearest, a mile away to the southeast, were the Inner Farne and the Wideopens. There was an old tower on the Farne, an ancient monastic building according to the book, and a white lighthouse that worked automatically and was visited only once a fortnight. To the northeast, nearly two miles away, were several more low-lying dots—Staple Island and the Brownsman, the Harcars and the Wamses, the Knivestone and the Longstone, with the lighthouse that Grace Darling had once made famous. They all seemed very remote, and I could make out so little detail through my own glasses that I had no fear any lighthouse keeper or bird watcher or visitor would notice me. From any of these bits of land, I would be a speck upon a speck. I had chosen my retreat well.

All the same, I knew it would be unwise to count absolutely on remaining undiscovered. *Shelduck's* black hull provided almost perfect camouflage against the rock, but there was always the outside chance that some fishing boat or yacht might pass sufficiently close to spot her, and I must be ready to meet the contingency. I must appear to have done everything that a reasonable man would have done to attract attention—and for anything left undone I must have a good explanation.

The first step, obviously, was to fly some signal of distress—and that was easy to arrange. I fetched my fishing rod from the boat and tied a white rag to the business end of it and propped it up with stones near the top of the rock. I fixed it at a drooping angle, knowing that no one who saw it would suppose it had been like that all the time. Against the white rock and the pale sky it was, I felt sure, quite invisible at any distance.

Now came the ticklish question of a fire. Naturally I didn't want to light one if I could help it, but it was certainly one of the things a stranded sailor would think of at once. Anyone arriving here during the next day or two might well be surprised if there were no ring of ashes at the top of the island. As the tide fell, I set off round the base of the rocks to survey my fuel resources. They turned out to be gratifyingly slender. There was no driftwood. There was nothing combustible at all except seaweed, and that would need a lot of drying before it would even give off a smoke signal. I was left, in fact, with the boat and its meager, carefully chosen contents. The loose floor boards in the cockpit and cabin would burn, but that was about all. Would I, I asked myself, have burned the floor boards at this stage if I had been a genuine castaway? I decided that I wouldn't—that it would have been a premature, panicky step. After all, I had food and water for a fortnight and a place to sleep, so I was far from desperate. I would have hoped to contrive, perhaps, some way of using the boat again. I would certainly have waited to see if my distress signal worked, or if I could attract the attention of a fishing vessel. In the meantime, I could show that a fire was in my mind by drying seaweed and preparing some kindling.

I fetched a jackknife from the boat and cut an armful or two of weed and spread it out conspicuously on the upper rocks. Then I set to work to whittle one of the smaller and more expendible floor boards into thin slivers. It was hard on the hands and on the knife blade, but I persisted, and presently I had a sizable heap of chips. Now I should be able to look any sudden rescuer in the face.

All this activity had made me hungry, and as the sun went down I prepared my first meal. I had bread, bacon, and sausages among my extra stores, and I decided to enjoy them while they were fresh. In a day or two I would be relying solely on tins—mostly fish and meat, eked out with biscuits and chocolate and a few oddments. I had purposely planned my diet on a frugal basis, for the less well fed I looked when I got ashore the better for my story. It would be a hardship to be always a little hungry, but a supportable one.

By the time I'd finished eating it was almost dark. I got out my thickest ropes and secured the boat fore and aft to spurs of rock. The wind was still light, and I didn't think she'd move much on the night tide, but by way of an extra precaution I brought the bower anchor ashore and wedged it in a rock cleft and drew the cable tight. Then, tired out after my exciting and strenuous day, I unrolled my sleeping bag and turned in.

Chapter Eight

My life on the Megstone during the days that followed was uneventful but very far from dull. In the best castaway tradition I made a mark on a rock each morning when I rose, and it was surprising how quickly the scratches mounted up. The fact that, at a pinch, I could leave the island any time I wished was the ultimate safeguard against tedium. I was lucky with the weather too in those early days, and I felt wonderfully fit and relaxed. I did the few chores around the boat, lingered over my sketchy meals, pottered about the rocks, cut more seaweed, and—whenever possible—swam and sunbathed. There was, I discovered, a deep gully near the south side of the island, which at high tide almost cut the place in two and at low tide made a perfect swimming pool. It was a spot much favored by gray seals, and I often came upon them basking there. The water was cold, but the sheltered ledges above it were hot in the sun, and I soon acquired a fine tan all over.

I spent hours watching the birds. They visited, or at least approached, the island in great variety—gulls and terns, razorbills and eider duck, even the occasional puffin—but guillemots and cormorants seemed to make up the bulk of the permanent colony. I never ceased to be fascinated by the black-and-bronze cormorants—weird, pre-historic-looking creatures at close quarters, which gobbled huge quantities of fish each day and dried themselves afterwards with outstretched wings like something on a coat of arms. They were silent birds, apart from an occasional harsh croak, yet there always seemed to be a commotion of some sort at the top of the rock where they gathered. Judging by the interesting courtships that were going on, it wouldn't be long before nesting started there, and then I'd be able to add those much-needed eggs to my menu. But there were none yet, and I avoided the place as far as possible, for it was running with limewash and stank to heaven.

When I had had enough of the birds, I could always watch the mainland shore. There was little movement on the coast road, but as April advanced and the warm weather continued a few people began to come down to the beaches in the middle of the day, and though they were no more than dots in the distance they gave me just enough sense of companionship to keep melancholy away. In the evenings and on the rare wet days I retired to *Shelduck's* cabin and listened to the radio, turned down low. I slept a good deal, and I thought a good deal—mostly pleasant thoughts. I felt none of the tension that I imagined must go with even the mildest criminal enterprise. Being still uncommitted, I didn't feel that I *was* engaged in a criminal enterprise. The outside possibility that I might one day have Isobel to myself as a result of what I was doing was never entirely absent from my mind, but I certainly wasn't counting any financial chickens, and I still preferred to look on my adventure as a diverting experiment, an entertaining hoax. The thought of the rumpus that must be breaking out over my disappearance, and of how wrong so many self-righteous people were going to be about me, afforded me an immense amount of quiet satisfaction. It was juvenile, no doubt, but I'd been associating too long with solemn and pompous men.

By now I had quite lost the feeling that someone might appear round the corner of the rock at any moment. It was pretty obvious that no one would, since there was nothing whatever to come for. Coastal steamers sometimes passed through the sound between the island and the mainland, but they kept their distance on account of the outlying rocks and would scarcely have seen me if I'd waved from the summit. The larger ships avoided the islands altogether. I saw one or two fishing boats, but their favorite grounds seemed to be farther out, and I never felt in danger from them. There was a little traffic between Seahouses and the bigger islands—the out-of-season visitor, perhaps, and the lighthouse service boats—but I was well off the track of it. By June, no doubt, with crowds of eager holiday makers milling around and keen to see all the sights, it would be a different story—particularly this year. The Megstone might yet become as famous as Grace Darling's Longstone! For the moment, though, I was perfectly safe.

I had no serious anxieties at all, in fact. *Shelduck*, perched up on her ledge, had been deserted by the sea soon after the stranding, just as I'd foreseen, and except for one roughish night when heavy spray blew in over her was as dry and secure as a house. I no longer troubled myself about whether I ought to light a fire at this stage or not, since I no longer feared interruption. My only real concern was my voracious, unsatisfied appetite. The keen sea air and my active life had given it a razor edge, and I often felt that I could have polished off the contents of the remaining tins at a single session. However, I had the consolation of seeing that my cheeks were becoming interestingly hollow under their vigorous growth of beard.

As the days passed, I began to look forward with a lively sense of expectation to hearing news about myself on the radio. The way I'd worked things out, I thought the first mention of me would probably come at the beginning of the second week. I wouldn't have been missed until the Tuesday when I'd been due back at the office, and to start with it would merely have been assumed that for some reason I'd overstayed my leave. Serious inquiries probably wouldn't have begun until Wednesday, and there would have been no real hue and cry until someone had thought of approaching Lesley, and found out about the telegram, and started to put two and two together. A week, I thought, was the inside limit. As it happened, my calculations turned out to have been on the conservative side, for the first reference to me was broadcast on Friday evening in the six o'clock news. It was just a sentence to the effect that inquiries were being made into the whereabouts of Commander Clive Easton, who had been missing from his home since the week end—with brief biographical details, in case anyone had forgotten me. I got quite a kick out of it.

After that listened to all the bulletins. For a while they were disappointingly negative. There was still no information. . . . Inquiries were still on foot. . . . Either the investigation was proceeding very slowly or else the B.B.C. was being characteristically cautious. By Sunday morning, though, I had been traced to Berwick-on-Tweed, where I was known to have sent a telegram to a friend, and this time the bulletin included an extremely accurate description of me, from my soft felt hat downwards. There were no further developments overthe week end, but on Monday evening things suddenly hotted up. The First Lord, answering a question in the House of Commons that afternoon, had stated that some classified documents were missing from my office.

The radio treatment was still very circumspect, but by the middle of the second week it was clear that the story had broken in a big way. My disappearance had been lifted to second place in the bulletins. M.I.5 and Special Branch officers, it was stated, were investigating the possibility that I might have left the country; the Admiralty, while denying that the missing documents were vital to national defense, had admitted that they were of some importance. The newspapers, I imagined, must by now be in full cry.

It was gratifying to see how well my plans had worked out, and I began to wish that I'd made arrangements to stay longer on the island. With each passing day the colunmists were likely to become less inhibited about me, and it seemed a pity not to give them rope. But I had only a few tins of food left, and my store of water was almost exhausted. The time was very near when I must leave.

I still hoped to avoid the long swim to the mainland. For some days I'd been considering the possibility that I might patch up *Shelduck* sufficiently to be able to use her as a raft. With fair weather and an easterly breeze, I thought, I'd have a good chance of being blown ashore. But when the spring tides began to come round again, I realized they weren't going to be high enough to float her—so that was that.

The alternative was to make an effective signal. I decided that I would have a huge fire, a real beacon of a blaze, on top of the rock on Friday night, using all *Shelduck's* floor boards and locker doors for fuel, as well as my stack of seaweed. If I lit the beacon after dark there was a fair chance that someone would see it and that the rock would be visited either during the night or early in the morning. In any case, I had to have a fire before I left, for I could then say it had been only the last of several, and no one would know better. If I failed to attract attention, I would swim ashore—weather permitting—at low water on Saturday evening, when the sea would be at its quietest and the distance at its shortest.

Then on Friday evening I began to make things ready for my departure. Newspapermen would undoubtedly be swarming over the rock before long, and everything they found must tell a convincing and consistent story. I climbed to the summit, and with birds screaming and circling all around me I adjusted the drooping fishing-rod signal so that at last it stood upright. A few yards away I set up a second signal, consisting of two of *Shelduck's* floor boards lashed together, with a shirt tied round one end. I had another look at the broken petrol tank connection and tinkered with it a bit until I was quite satisfied that the damage looked accidental. I even put stones in some of the empty food tins and hurled them out into deep water, in case anyone should think that I had been suspiciously well provided for. When I had assured myself that everything was in order, I gathered up an armful of dry seaweed from *Shelduck's* cockpit and set off once more for the top of the rock to choose a site for the fire.

I was just coming up to the skyline when I saw something that I hadn't seen in the whole two weeks I'd been there—a fishing boat so close in that I could almost have thrown one of my tins into it. Instinctively—and quite forgetting in that second that I was now ready to leave—I ducked and half-turned away. Then it happened! My foot slipped on a slimy surface, and with my arms full of weed I hadn't a chance to save myself. I fell heavily, and as I hit the ground a spur of rock jabbed savagely into my back. The blow completely winded me, and for a while I lay there gasping and helpless. The pain was so agonizing that at first I was afraid I might have done some serious damage to myself, and as soon as

I'd got my breath back I made an effort to sit up. To my relief I managed it, though only with the greatest difficulty. I tried, with what voice I had, to hail the fishing boat, but it must have passed on, for there was no response and I could no longer hear its engine. Feeling horribly sick and weak, I began to lower myself down the slope, foot by torturing foot, until at last, after what seemed an age of crawling, I succeeded in reaching *Shelduck*.

Chapter Nine

I had a shocking night. I swallowed some aspirin to dull the pain, but I still couldn't sleep. I tried sitting up, curling up, lying flat—but it made no difference. By morning I was a wreck. As soon as it grew light I had a look at my back with the help of a mirror, and there was a bruise as big as a dinner plate at the base of the spine, with an ugly contused cut where the point of rock had driven into the flesh. I was so stiff I could scarcely move. Far from being in a condition to swim to the mainland, I couldn't even hope to climb to the top of the rock in my present state! I had become, willy-nilly, a genuine castaway, with no means whatever of getting off this island that I'd so lightheartedly marooned myself upon. It was an unnerving thought, but I couldn't help appreciating the irony of the situation. It looked as though I was going to earn any rewards there might ultimately be by much sterner sacrifices than I'd dreamed of.

I mentally reviewed the stores position—and it didn't take long. I had one small tin of corned beef, a fragment of chocolate, and about a dozen biscuits. That was bad enough; but the water position was still more disquieting. There were about three pints left in the bottom of the can, and after my restless night I already had a raging thirst. Even with the most rigorous self-denial, those few cupfuls would hardly last more than a day or so. Rain would save me, but at present there was no sign of any. Meanwhile, rest seemed to be the only thing—rest for my back, and a careful conservation of strength, so that at the earliest possible moment I could get on with building the fire that was now my only hope. I passed a long, grim day, relieved only in part by the companionship of the radio.

Even that would soon be denied me, for the battery was beginning to run low.

The pain was slightly easier when I woke up on Sunday morning, but I was still very much of a cripple, and I knew I couldn't attempt to carry fuel to the summit that day. It was all I could do to crawl out of the boat. I sat on the ledge in the sun, eating the last crumbs of corned beef and biscuit and washing them down with a spoonful or two of water. Then I struggled over to a pool and bathed my aching back. There were limpets on the rocks, and I tried to chip some of them off with a sharp stone. At first I wasn't very successful, but the knack came with practice, and soon I had half a dozen prized away. They were deliciously succulent, but afterwards they made me thirstier than ever—and by now I was down to my last cup of water. The effort had tired me, too, and presently I had to return to the cabin. I lay there for a long time, trying to think up some new way of attracting attention. I wondered if it would be worth while to light a fire on the ledge beside the boat, which was as far as I could hope to carry anything that day. Only a passing ship would be able to see it, and from a ship it would no doubt appear to be on the mainland—but it seemed better than doing nothing. As darkness fell I took a pile of wood chips ashore and set light to them. I fed the fire with dry seaweed, and for a time it burned well, but nothing else happened. In the end I decided it was a waste of valuable fuel and gave it up.

By next morning, with no food or water left, I knew that I had to do something about the summit beacon even if it killed me. I took a floor board from the cockpit and set off up the uneven slope on my hands and knees, dragging the board behind me. Every move was excruciating, and the climb seemed endless. For me, this pimple of a hill had become an Everest. When at last I reached the top, the sweat of pain was streaming from my face. I left the plank among the weed and flotsam that the cormorants had begun to bring in for their nests and returned to the boat for another one. The second trip was still more exhausting and took me a full half hour. This time, before I left, I collected my fishing rod. I hadn't tried to fish while things were going well, for there was no good bait on the island, but now in my extremity I wondered if limpets would serve. I slid the rod over the rocks ahead of me and started to crawl after it. I thought I was doing fine, but on the way down I suddenly passed out. For the moment, at any rate, I'd reached my limit. I dragged myself back to the boat and slumped onto the bunk, completely spent.

Later, when I'd recovered a little, I made my way to a ledge that overhung a deep pool and tried my luck with the rod. I kept at it for an hour but caught nothing. In the end I couldn't bear to look at the cool, tantalizing water any longer. My mouth was so dry that I could scarcely swallow, and my tongue felt like a piece of pumice. I knew that people *had* drunk sea water and survived, but I didn't trust it—or myself, once I'd started—and I was determined to put off the moment as long as possible. A slight fall in the barometer encouraged me to wait.

That night I dreamed of *scampi* and *coq au vin* and a bottle of cold Chablis. It was a lovely dream—and a horrible awakening. I felt like death. I eased my tight and aching throat with a few limpets from my store, but they did little to assuage my torturing thirst. As soon as day-light came I staggered down to the sea and lay with my face in the surf and my mouth open, letting the bitter water wash over my parched lips and swollen tongue. I swallowed a little, and then dragged myself away with a rending effort of will and started at once to carry the rest of the wood and the dry seaweed to the top of the rock. My back was less painful, and I knew I had to finish the job while I could. I toiled all morning, and by midday everything that would burn was at the summit. I left it in a heap where I'd dumped it. I would build the fire towards evening, I decided, and light it at dusk. The prospect gave me strength to bear my thirst a little longer. It was going to be a good fire, a really tremendous fire. Someone was bound to see it. Tomorrow, I told myself, a boat would come and the torment would be over. I ate some more limpets and lay down in the cabin and hied to empty my mind of all thoughts.

I must have slept, for the next thing I was aware of was the gentle patter of rain on the roof. In an instant I had scrambled from my sleeping bag and rushed into the cockpit. The cabin top was glistening, and I bent and sucked greedily at the wet canvas. As the drops fell faster I fetched a cup and held it at the corner of the dripping roof until I had enough to roll around my tongue. I thrust the cup back under the quickening stream and waited until it was a quarter full and then took a real draught. It was ecstasy. Now my only fear was that the shower would stop before I could gather enough for my needs. With frantic haste I collected bowls and saucepans and pails and placed them in strategic spots to catch the rivulets. But the rain grew heavier and turned into a downpour, and they filled quickly. Soon my water can was brimming, and I knew I need worry no more. The long thirst was over.

It was only then that I remembered the fire! All my work of the morning, all my precious fuel, had gone for nothing. By now the wood and the weed must be soaked through and through.

There was worse to come. For the next three days it rained almost incessantly, and the wind rose to a near gale. The sea was a tossing gray waste, and though the tides were only just past neaps, at each high water the waves crashed and pounded against *Shelduck's* hull with such violence that I feared she might be swept away. I continued to gather limpets in the brief lulls, and once I climbed to the summit of the rock in the hope that I might be able to knock some bird on the head, but the unsuccessful effort cost me more strength than I could afford, and I didn't try it again. I could feel myself growing weaker each day, and for the first time I began seriously to wonder if I should ever get off this cursed rock. It seemed fantastic that a man might actually *die* here, a mere couple of miles from land, but I'd laid my plans only too well. No one knew where I was except Isobel, so I could expect no help unless it came from her. She must be getting a little worried by now, for according to my tale of scratches on the rock I was more than a week overdue. If she was worried enough, she might decide to tell all and face the scandal and humiliation. She *might*. With a life at stake, it would be a small thing to do—most women in her position wouldn't have hesitated. Somehow, though, I couldn't see Isobel making the sacrifice. And if she did nothing and the weather remained bad, death was a very real possibility. A stupid death, too. I would reconcile myself to it, of course, if I had to—just as I'd done when I'd first gone into submarines. I'd been prepared for it then—I'd assumed it might happen—I'd forced myself to believe that it didn't matter, that nothing mattered. Everyone has his defense, and that was mine—to seize the hour and be ready for the worst. I had no doubt I could recapture the mood. But I wasn't finished yet, and I had no intention of giving up without a struggle.

On the evening of the third day the glass steadied and the rain cleared, and I tottered feebly from my bunk. As I passed the mirror I caught sight of my reflection, and for a moment I gazed at myself in disbelief. I had once, I supposed, been good-looking in a jaded, disillusioned sort of way. Now I was a ghastly spectacle. My face was emaciated, my eyes bloodshot from the salt and wind, my lips cracked and puffy, my hair matted and unkempt. I looked like the Ancient Mariner himself! The sight shocked me, but it gave me the jolt I needed. Once more I toiled to the summit, ignoring the angry squawkings of the birds that rose all round me. Dusk was falling, and the surface of the rock was still wet, and this time I moved with care. I found the pile of saturated fuel and spread the seaweed and the wood chips out to dry and propped the floor boards against each other so that the breeze would blow around them. For the moment, there was nothing more I could do. I turned to recross the stinking, lime-washed peak, and as I took a first cautious step in the half-light my foot tangled with something on the ground. I bent down and saw it was a nest that I'd kicked and scattered. Then I noticed the egg!—gleaming, chalky white, as big as a hen's egg. I grabbed it and broke the shell on my teeth and emptied the contents down my throat. It was strong and fishy, but I thought it the most luscious and reviving thing I'd ever tasted. Eagerly I searched around for more. There was one that had fallen down a fissure in the rock and smashed there, and I cursed my clumsiness in upsetting the nest. But soon I found others—the cormorants had evidently been busy during my enforced stay below. I drank the contents of two more, filled my pockets, and returned to the boat. I made a little fire of wood chips, beat up half a dozen eggs, and made a sort of omelet. With warm, solid food in my stomach, hope returned. Judging by the number of birds I'd put up during my sortie, there must be a lot more eggs up there. It looked as though my luck had turned.

I still thought so next day, for there was a steady breeze and plenty of sunshine, and most of the fuel dried quickly. By the afternoon I was ready to build my fire. The best site seemed to be the place where I'd scattered the nest the previous night, for the long fissure would help the draft. I laid the foundations carefully, using the floor-board shavings and some odd scraps of paper as tinder, and piling the robbed birds' nests, the dry seaweed, and the planks on top of it. At four in the afternoon I put a match to it.

It burned slowly at first. I'd been a little too impatient, and the planks were wetter than I'd thought. But it gave off quite a lot of smoke, and as the evening wore on it began to glow with a red heart. I tended it for a while and then went down to the boat and watched it from there. Several times it burst into flickering flames, and once, for a short time, there was a fine blaze. Still it was far from being the beacon that I'd planned. Tired out and rather dispirited, I turned in at last and left it to burn.

There was still life in it in the morning, and after I'd added some freshly cut weed it began to send up a thin plume of smoke. But the damp weed made poor fuel, and I couldn't imagine the smoke ever becoming a really efficient signal. To make matters worse, a thick sea fog started to roll in over the rock around noon. I felt very low. It was obvious that the fire hadn't been noticed during the night, or someone would have come by now. There was no chance at all that anyone would see it while the fog lasted. I had no hope of another big night blaze, for I'd burned all my wood. If I'd had an ax I could have broken up the boat, but I'd deliberately refrained from bringing one. So what now? The cormorants wouldn't go on providing me with food forever. My back was getting better, but I was much too weak to think of swimming two miles. There was a possibility that some visitor might want to see the rock soon, since it was now May and the season must be starting, but I couldn't bank on it. That plume of smoke seemed, after all, to be my best hope, and I'd got to keep it going.

In the middle of the afternoon I took some more weed to the summit and flung it on the smouldering heap. I was about to set off down the hill again when I thought I caught the sound of an engine. I listened, and was sure of it. It seemed unusually near—and it was getting nearer. I peered into the fog, which had begun to thin in places. At fist I could see nothing. Then a dark shape slowly emerged. It was an open launch with two shrouded figures in it. It appeared to be heading straight for the Megstone. . . . It *was* heading for the Megstone!

I suddenly went crazy with excitement. Someone must have seen the fire after all. *I'd done it!*

I waved frantically and began to shout, in a cracked voice that I hardly recognized as my own. I kept on waving, and presently the man in the bows spotted me and waved back. He was wearing a flat peaked cap and a blue overcoat, and as the boat drew nearer I saw that he was a policeman. I couldn't understand that. A fire on the Megstone would have brought a coastguardman—perhaps even the lifeboat—but not a policeman. Perhaps it wasn't the fire that had brought them—perhaps Isobel *had* told everything, after all! I didn't care, anyway—I was too far gone to care. Rescue was all. As the launch chugged slowly in to the island I turned and descended the rocky slope for the last time.

Chapter Ten

There was too much swell for the launch to come right in, even on the lee side, but she had a dinghy in tow, and the policeman, a solidly built, gray-haired sergeant, rowed himself to a sheltered inlet and scrambled ashore. As he drew near me, he stared as though I were some apparition.

"Commander Easton?" he said. There were disbelief and awe in his voice—but no trace of hostility.

I nodded.

"Well, I'll be damned!" He looked at *Shelduck*, he looked at the limpet shells and eggshells scattered all round her, he looked up at the smouldering fire on the summit, and he looked again at me. "Are you all right, sir?"

"More or less."

He was obviously bursting with questions, but sensibly he didn't ask them. "Well, we'd better get you out of it," he said. He produced a flask from the side pocket of his coat. "Here, drink some of this—it'll do you good." I took the flask, and it was full of hot coffee laced with brandy. I'd almost forgotten that such comforts existed. I sipped it slowly while he went aboard *Shelduck* and packed my bag. Then, in a dour Scottish silence thickened by incredulity, he helped me into the dinghy and rowed me to the launch. The boatman nodded to me, goggling. He seemed totally deprived of speech.

I was still very much in the dark myself. As we set off in the direction of Seahouses, I said, "What brought you, Sergeant?—did you see the fire?"

He shook his head. "Not till we'd almost got here. It was the bottle with your message in it."

I nearly said "What bottle?" but I bit the words off just in time. "Ah!" I said, and waited.

"Washed up this morning, it was, at Bamburgh."

Light began to dawn. I couldn't for the life of me imagine how Isobel had done it, but if a bottle had been found with a message from me in it, she was obviously the only person who could have fixed it. I might have been right about her reluctance to sacrifice herself, but it was clear that I'd grossly underrated her initiative. . . . I gave a noncommittal nod. The less I said the better, till I knew a bit more.

By now the sergeant couldn't contain his own curiosity any longer. "What happened, sir?" he asked. "How on earth did you come to get stuck like that?"

I told him in a couple of hundred well-chosen words. He kept shaking his head from side to side. "Och, there's going to be some trouble over this," he said. He continued to stare at me. "What do you want to do when you get ashore? Shall I take you along to the hospital?"

"There's no need for that," I told him. "I'll be all right once I've got a bit of food inside me."

"The hotel, maybe?"

"Will they have me like this?"

"Aye, they'll have you."

I nodded again and let my chin sink on my chest. I didn't have to pretend to be exhausted.

The news had begun to get around, and there was a little knot of people on the quay. The sergeant and a young constable helped me ashore, while the bystanders gazed at me in fascinated silence. A flash bulb went off, and a solitary reporter stepped forward and said he was from the local paper. I muttered something incoherent, and the sergeant waved him away. He'd got his scoop, though. That picture of the Ancient Mariner straight from the sea would be worth a lot very soon.

A police car was waiting, and in a few minutes I was being received into the King's Head in an atmosphere of hushed efficiency. The proprietress, Mrs. Oliver, personally delivered a light meal to my room in no time at all, and I ate it before I washed. Afterwards I soaked myself in hot water, shedding the grime of weeks and gloriously easing my stiff back. I decided the beard must stay for the time being, but I tidied it up a bit and changed into my decent suit of clothes, and I thought I looked reasonably presentable. Presently the sergeant came up to my room with a doctor from the village, a young, competent Scot. He'd heard a bit of the story, and the questions he asked me were strictly professional. He gave me a routine examination, asked me what I'd found to eat, and tut-tutted a little over my bruised back. He didn't seem at all alarmed. He said I must have a fine constitution and that I hadn't taken any real harm, but I'd better go easy with the food at first and get plenty of rest, and the back might need some massage later. I thanked him, and said I'd have it looked at again in London.

When he'd gone, the sergeant—his name was Framley—produced a brown paper parcel. "I thought you might like to have this, sir, as a memento."

I opened it and uncovered a pint beer bottle. There was a roll of paper inside the bottle—a page torn from a Fontana thriller. It had evidently been inserted as a loose spill and allowed to spring open inside, so that it pressed tightly against the glass. Penciled across it in large, thick black capitals were the words I'M MAROONED ON MEGSTONE. HELP! CLIVE EASTON.

I grinned at Framley. "Good job I drink beer!"

"You were very lucky," he said solemnly.

"Who found it?"

"A lad named Alan Granger. He's up from London to stay with his grannie at Bamburgh, and he found it while he was playing on the beach this morning. He took it home with him, and his grannie brought it round to the station after dinner. We thought someone was playing a joke, of course—but I said we'd better not chance it."

"I'm more than grateful to you for that, Sergeant. And to the boy, too—I'll have to see him before I go. . . . Anyway, thanks for the bottle, I'd like to keep it. And now I suppose I'd better start letting people know I've come back to life. . . ."

Framley broke in, "If you take my advice, sir, you'll have a good long rest while you've got the chance. There'll be all hell breaking loose before long."

"What do you mean?"

He regarded me curiously. "Don't you know what they've been saying about you? I thought with that radio aboard ..."

"You mean that nonsense about my leaving the country? Yes, I heard that—I thought it was a damned outrage. . . . You don't mean people have taken it seriously?"

"Very seriously indeed, sir. You've been in all the papers for weeks. Everybody knows about you—you're a sort of—well, a national figure, sir. Not a very popular one, I'm afraid."

"Good God!"

"The reporters'll be up here in droves, you can be sure of that. The best thing you can do, sir, is to get to bed and have a good long sleep, the way the doctor said, and I'll post a man downstairs to keep everybody off till morning. Then you can decide what to do."

I considered for a moment, and it seemed a good idea. "That's very nice of you, Sergeant," I said. "I think I'll take you up on it."

I slept for fifteen hours, and when I woke I felt ready for anything. I rang the bell, and Mrs. Oliver answered it herself. She looked, I thought, a trifle harassed. She asked me how I'd slept and what I'd like for breakfast, and I said porridge and rolls and coffee, in bed.

"And a nice egg?" she suggested.

"No eggs!" I said firmly.

"There's this message for you, sir, from a gentleman downstairs. Urgent, he said it was." She gave me an envelope and departed. I opened it and took the slip of paper out, and it said: "I am instructed by the Editor of the *Daily Gazette* to offer you £5,000 for your exclusive story." It was signed "G. M. Fellowes."

It was tempting, of course—and I couldn't imagine what Isobel would say if she ever learned I'd refused it. All the same, I knew this wasn't the moment to start grabbing. I was too unsure of my ground. I wrote across it, "Please thank your Editor, but there's nothing I wish to sell," and put it back in the envelope. When Mrs. Oliver came up with the tray I gave it to her.

"Is there anyone else down there?" I said.

She gave me an odd look. "There are sixty-three gentlemen from the press having breakfast on the lawn," she said.

"Heavens!" I took a deep breath. "All right, Mrs. Oliver, I'll be down soon."

As soon as she'd gone I got out of bed and went over to the window. The square outside the hotel, which the day before had been almost completely deserted, now looked like a city parking lot. There were scores of vehicles, including two or three police cars. Blue uniforms were everywhere—half the Northumberland constabulary seemed to have been drafted in for the occasion. Two newsreel trucks were maneuvering into position at the edge of the congested lawn. Alert-looking young men in towny clothes were moving among the cars. Around the square the doors of houses and shops stood open, and little groups of people were waiting about in expectant attitudes. It looked as though Seahouses was going to have quite a day!

I breakfasted slowly and rather thoughtfully. I'd had something to do with the press after the *Wilhelm II* affair, but then the Ministry of Information had handled the whole show. Now I was on my own. It was encouraging that the interest should be so great, but I'd have to watch my step. I spent some time mentally revising the story I'd originally intended to tell, in the light of later events.

I'd just finished dressing when there was a tap at the door, and Mrs. Oliver looked in again. "There's a gentleman here to see you, sir ..." she said. I wondered who it could be who had managed to slip through Sergeant Framley's cordon, and thought of M.I.5. Then George Grey's solemn face appeared in the doorway.

"My *dear* fellow ...!" he exclaimed, advancing quickly upon me with outstretched hand. "This is quite, *quite* incredible...."

He went on wringing my hand and saying how incredible it was and how delighted he was and what an appalling time I must have had for quite a while. It was the nearest thing to strong emotion days afterwards I could scarcely stir out of the cabin. It was during this time that I had the idea of putting a message in a bottle, though it seemed a very long shot and I didn't really believe it would work. My main hope was that once I could move around again I'd be able to use the charred fragments of wood left by the first fire to start another one, and then keep it fed with seaweed until someone saw the smoke, but the weather turned bad and it rained for three days almost without a break, and it wasn't until the day before yesterday that I managed to get the fire started again. Even then it didn't amount to much. The last of my food had run out and I was very weak and—well, quite frankly, I thought I'd had it. Then a boat suddenly appeared—and here I am!"

I looked at Grey, and he gave me an approving nod and asked if there were any questions.

There were lots of questions! They pressed me for every kind of detail. They wanted to know much more about the food angle, and I explained that after my coastal trip I'd had a few stores left over, which had lasted me nearly a fortnight, and I gave them a rough inventory. I told them about the limpets, and about my unsuccessful attempts to fish and to knock over a cormorant, and of the joy it had been to taste the first birds' eggs just before my rescue. They asked about water, and I told them of the frightful straits I'd been in before the storm broke and how I'd already begun to drink a little sea water. They asked me about boats passing nearby, and I said I'd seen quite a few at different times but that they'd always given the island a wide berth. They asked me how I'd occupied my time and whether I'd had anything to read and whether I'd kept a log, and I said I'd been too worried about keeping alive to keep a log and that I'd had only one paperback book, which I'd torn up to get the last fire going, but that I had had a portable radio. One of them said that in that case I must have heard what was being said about me, and I said I'd nothing at all to say about that at this stage. They asked me how I'd reached the boat from Berwick, and I told them about the bus, and one of them said it was surprising that no one had remembered me after the inquiries had started, and I explained that I'd changed into my

I'd ever seen him display. Apparently he'd heard the news late the previous evening and had come straight up on the night train. He'd been piecing things together downstairs with the help of Sergeant Framley, but now of course he wanted to hear the whole story, and I gave him my revised version in full. It was a useful rehearsal, and I thought I got through it pretty well. He was staggered by my adventures and horrified at the privations I'd suffered, but he accepted my account without question. Then it was his turn. He said he understood I knew about the accusations that had been made against me. I said I did, and asked him what on earth had started people thinking along those lines, and he said it was my telegram to Lesley Ashe—and, of course, the documents. I said, oh yes, I'd heard something on the radio about some missing documents but the reception had been bad and what was it all about? He explained rather sheepishly that some documents *had* been missing from my room but that they'd been found a couple of days ago in "J" file, where I must have put them by mistake. I said in that case it looked as though I'd only myself to thank and that I was sorry about it and deserved a bawling-out for being so careless, and he gave me a thin smile and said he thought I'd had all the bawlings-out that were necessary. He assured me, with only a trace of embarrassment, that he personally had felt all the time that there must be some other explanation of my disappearance. I made it clear in my turn that I realized I'd behaved like a damn fool in letting my private affairs get me down, which was the thing that had really started all the trouble, but he said anyone could get into a bad nervous state and he didn't think I need blame myself on that score. He admitted he'd been a little perturbed about some of the political remarks I was supposed to have let drop. I asked him what remarks, and he quoted a few of them, and I said they'd been distorted and that I'd certainly never even been pink, let alone red. In any case, I said, they'd merely been a reflection of my private frustration and bad temper and had never been intended to be taken seriously. He seemed to find my explanation reasonable enough. He said that no doubt I'd be taking some action about the newspapers in due course, and I said I'd have to see first exactly what they'd written about me. He said, with an expression of distaste, that while he hadn't himself read the more lurid pieces he could tell me that they'd written a good deal!

I said, "Well, judging by the activity downstairs, it looks as though they want to write a good deal more! What am I going to do about all those chaps? If I don't talk to them they'll just about tear the place down."

"Oh, you'll have to say something," he agreed. "It's irregular, of course, but the circumstances are unique and I'm sure the Board won't object if you stick to the bare facts and keep it short. . . . Do you feel fit enough, though?"

"I'm fine," I said. "Shall we go down and get it over?"

By now a police superintendent had taken charge of the arrangements. He met us at the bottom of the stairs and personally conducted us into the garden, where the reporters were marshaled. At a rough glance, I'd have said there were more like a hundred of them than sixty. As I limped into view there was a sudden, startled hush. Then they surged forward, and camera bulbs began flashing, and for a few moments I stood there half-blinded and let them flash.

Presently Grey raised his hand and said in his quiet but compelling chairman's voice, "Gentlemen, let's try to keep this conference as orderly as possible, shall we? Commander Easton has had an extremely bad time, as you can see, but he's ready to tell you his story if you'll let him take things at his own pace."

There was a murmur of sympathy and assent. A policeman brought me a deck chair, and as soon as I'd made myself comfortable I started to talk. I touched briefly and casually on the background to the story—how I'd taken a holiday trip up the coast in March in a friend's boat, and left it in a sheltered bay not far from Bamburgh because the weather had turned bad, and rejoined it in April for a long week end. Then I said:

"My idea was to spend the Saturday afternoon cruising round the islands and put in here for the night and perhaps go out again on Sunday. Unfortunately it didn't work out like that. I was just

off the Megstone when I smelt petrol more strongly than I to have done. I had a look at the connectious and discovere the union nut under the tap was leaking rather badly. I spanner and started to fix it, but I must have strained at th too hard because the whole pipe suddenly broke away fro tank and the petrol poured out. The engine stopped at on course, and the boat began to drift. There was a steady b blowing in from the sea and I thought that with a bit of luc be carried ashore—but instead I was set straight onto the Megs and stranded there at the top of the tide."

I paused. There wasn't a sound in the garden but the scratc pencils and the quick flicking over of pages. They weren't mis a thing. After a moment I continued:

"I didn't feel particularly worried—I thought it would be e enough to attract someone's attention. I rigged up a distress sig on the top of the rock, and as soon as it got dark I lit a fire th too. I hadn't a lot of fuel—mainly the floor boards of the boat a some damp seaweed—but I used all I had. It promised to be splendid fire, and I was sure someone would see it and come a take me off. But my luck was out—I'd just about got it going wh a sea fog started to creep in, and it must have persisted all nig because the fire wasn't noticed. At least—no one came."

I took a sip of water from a glass that someone had place beside me, and went on:

"I still wasn't too worried. I hoped I'd be able to get the boa off on the next afternoon's tide and make the shore somehow. Bu when the time came I found I couldn't shove her clear of the rock because of the surf and the pressure of the wind against her hull Conditions got better later on, but by then it was impossible to move her because the tides had begun to take off and she'd been left high and dry on the ledge where she'd grounded.

"I really did seem to be stuck, now—but the worst was still to come. I was constantly going up to the top of the rock to see if there was anyone about and to prop up my signal, which kept getting blown over by the wind—and on my way down one evening I fell heavily and bruised my back. The pain was so bad that for

boat clothes in Berwick because I had to cross a lot of mud and I didn't want to get my decent things filthy, and they took the point. No one seemed to know about the dinghy, and I thought it unnecessary to mention it myself.

On the whole, they were very restrained and considerate, and there certainly wasn't any breath of suspicion in the way they angled their questions. I think they were all rather inhibited by their knowledge of what their papers had written about me and their feeling that I was a deeply injured man. There were a lot of things, too, that they'd already got straightened out from other sources. They didn't ask about the telegram, or the documents, or mention the Polish steamer, or refer at all to my state of health before I'd got stranded, or to my personal affairs. All these things, I realized, had now been accepted as irrelevancies. Right at the end one man did say, "Have you been in touch with Miss Ashe, sir?" but I withered him with a curt "No comment!" and Grey decided that that was a suitable moment to close the conference. It had really gone very well indeed.

Grey left for London soon afterwards, having assured me that it would be perfectly all right for me to take indefinite sick leave and report back for work only when I felt quite fit again. Most of the reporters, too, faded away after the conference, and I gathered they'd hired fishing boats and gone out to the Megstone to take pictures and get material for descriptive pieces about my life there, just as I'd foreseen. Some late-comers continued to arrive, however, and what with answering supplementary questions and dealing with telephone calls I decided that the sooner I got back to town myself the better. Besides, I was eager to see Isobel and get her end of the story.

First, though, I had a duty call to make on Master Alan Granger, the bottle finder. Sergeant Framley insisted on driving me over to Bamburgh as I had no transport of my own. The house was a small detached villa in a quiet lane called The Wynding, overlooking the empty stretch of sandy beach and dunes on the north side of the castle. One or two photographers were hanging about there, waiting for me.

I went in and paid my respects to Mrs. Granger, a vigorous and alert old lady. Then I turned my attention to the boy who'd helped to save my life. He was a pale, rather fragile-looking child, with big brown eyes and a shock of yellow hair over his forehead and an attractive, slow smile. He seemed a little overawed at first, but I soon put him at his ease, and after that we got on fine together. I learned that he was ten years old and that he lived in London and that he'd just had measles very badly and had been sent up to his grannie's to get as much sunshine and sea bathing as he could. He'd been at Bamburgh for three days, he said, and was going to be there for a month. I said his visit had certainly been a stroke of luck for me, and thanked him warmly for bringing the bottle home. I refrained from asking him any questions about how and where he'd found it. Instead, I plunged into a racy account of my adventures on the island, which he seemed to find very thrilling. Before I left, I gave him a pound to spend on his holiday and a check for ten pounds to take back to London with him. The photographers were keen to get pictures of us together, and we posed outside the front door, much to Alan's delight. Then I pushed off.

Back in Seahouses, I fixed up with a local fisherman to salvage *Shelduck* at the first suitable tide and keep her in the harbor until I'd decided what to do about her. I answered a few more questions at the hotel, thanked Mrs. Oliver for her kindness, allowed my firm friend Sergeant Framley to run me into Berwick, and caught the afternoon train to London.

Chapter Eleven

I arrived at King's Cross just before ten and rang the Cowleys' home from the station. Isobel answered the phone. Judging by the speed with which the receiver came off, she must have been waiting beside it. She sounded terrifically thrilled. She said Walter was abroad, and couldn't I come round right away? I said that nothing would stop me. I got a cab and dropped my things at the flat and walked straight over.

My heart was pumping pretty fast as I slipped in by the half-open door. Isobel was the pay-off for all that I'd gone through, and she had to be good—as good as the mental pictures of her that had helped to sustain me on the Megstone. And she was!—better! The moment I saw her, all the old craziness came back. I shoved the door to with my foot and grabbed her.

"Why, darling," she exclaimed, when she'd got her breath, "that's no way for a survivor to behave! And your beard!" She leaned back and surveyed me. "Heavens, you *are* in a state—positively all skin and bone!"

"You're not," I said, caressing her.

"Darling, don't . . . ! Tell me, how's the bruise?"

"Oh, much better."

"I'm so glad. It sounded quite incapacitating."

"I gather you've seen the papers?"

"Yes—it's all in the evenings. I've read the whole story. Was that really what happened to you?—what you told them?"

"More or less. I changed things round a bit, that's all."

"Was it *very* awful?"

She sounded as concerned as though she really cared, but it was sympathy without compassion and I didn't dwell.

"It could have been a lot worse," I said. "It *would* have been, if you hadn't rallied round."

She smiled her amused smile. "Well, I couldn't risk losing all that lovely money, could I . . .? Look, if you'll remove your hands for a moment I'll get you a drink."

I followed her into the drawing room. "That bottle was an inspiration," I said, "though I'm still not clear how you worked it."

She looked very smug. "It was really quite simple, darling. I got everything ready here first, and then I drove all through the night and reached that place, Bamburgh, about ten. I left the car in the sand dunes and found a good strategic spot under the castle where I could sit and watch the beach both ways without being very visible myself. You see, I knew it wouldn't be enough just to leave the bottle lying on the sand because it might not have been seen for ages—but as it happened I didn't have to. It was a glorious day before that horrible fog came up, and there were several people dotted about, and one of them was the boy. He'd been swimming, and he was sitting alone on the beach drying himself. I walked past him, and there were some flat rocks and a rock pool quite near. I put the bottle down so that the message was very conspicuous, and then I turned and walked slowly back to him and said, 'Have you seen that big crab?' and pointed, and of course he jumped up and went off to have a look."

"So that's how he came to find it!" I said. "Very clever!"

"That's what I thought."

"Was there a crab, by the way?"

"Naturally there was, darling. Perhaps it wasn't quite as big as I made out, but it was a perfectly good crab. . . . Anyway, I walked on quickly, and when I turned round again I could see he was holding the bottle and examining it, and presently he left the beach and went tearing up the road with it, so I knew everything would be all right. After that, I had a little nap in the sand dunes, and then I drove straight back here. Seven hundred miles in two days, believe it or not!"

"It must have been a hell of a trip for you," I said. I found it strange now to remember I'd once thought her languorous!

"I was absolutely dead, of course."

"Never mind, you've resurrected wonderfully."

She laughed. "Don't you think I did rather well?"

"I think you did quite remarkably. . . ." I sipped my whisky and silently weighed her achievement. After a while I said, "It's a pity, of course, that the boy had to see you. . . ."

"He only saw me for a second, and I'm sure he forgot all about me straight away."

"Probably. He certainly didn't mention you."

"Well, of course not, and he's not likely to, because he'll want to keep all the glory to himself. Wouldn't you, if you'd been made a little hero of?"

"I expect so. It's only that we've got to be quite satisfied we're in the clear as we go along. If anyone ever got suspicious . . ."

"Why on earth should they?"

"I don't suppose they will for a moment, but we can't be too careful. . . . Could anyone have seen you with the bottle?"

"Not a chance. I kept it in my handbag until the very last minute."

"You may have been noticed up there, all the same."

"I doubt it. I was dressed in a very ordinary way, and I didn't speak to a soul."

"You must have eaten somewhere?"

"I took sandwiches and a flask of coffee, and while I was there I picnicked."

"I see. . . . What about this end—did anyone know you were away from home? Had Walter left by then?"

"Yes, he left the day before I drove up. That was what I had to wait for—that was the awful part. You see, first of all, when you didn't turn up according to plan, I thought perhaps your food had lasted longer than you'd expected, and I could see that each extra day was an advantage to us. But after three weeks I was sure something must have gone wrong, and I felt dreadfully worried because I knew I was the only person who could do anything. I tried to think of a reason for leaving Walter, but it wasn't easy because it meant a whole day and a night away at the very least, and I never do leave him, and of course I didn't want to risk drawing attention to myself and what I was doing. Then, when I was practically at my wit's end, he suddenly said he'd got to go off to Belgium, doctor or no doctor, and that was that. What's more, darling—though I don't suppose it interests you much—he'll be away for another two weeks."

I gave a slightly preoccupied nod. "What about the woman who cleans here? Does she know you were away?"

"No—the day I was away was her day off. I thought of that."

"And what did you do with the book you tore the page out of?"

"I burned it in the stove. Relax, darling—everything's been taken care of."

I relaxed.

"Well," I said, "I congratulate you."

"That's a relief, anyway—I was beginning to wonder . . . ! In that case, I congratulate *you*. After all, it was you who put in most of the hard work."

"I'd say it's been a fine co-operative effort."

"Yes, and a productive one."

"It could be."

"But it's going to be, darling—things have gone marvelously. Wait until you see what the papers have been saying about you! The *Courier* was the worst—it found out about your string of girl friends and really went to town. 'This dissolute lecher,' I think they called you—something like that, anyway." She smiled mischievously. "I'm sure that's actionable, darling—don't they say the greater the truth the greater the libel? I think you ought to see your lawyer at once."

I laughed. "I'd sooner wait a few days and watch developments," I said. "There may be snags we don't know about."

"It all looks straightforward enough to me."

"I dare say, but there are one or two things I'd like to clear up. . . . Have you seen anything of Lesley?"

"Yes, quite a bit."

"How is she?"

"Well, she was very upset about you, of course, and she did have rather a sticky time with the newspapers, but she's all right, really. In fact, she's well on the way to acquiring a new boy friend."

"*Is* she!"

"At least, perhaps that's putting it the wrong way round—she isn't doing much about it herself yet, because she *was* rather smitten with you, but he's certainly fallen for her in a big way."

"Well, this is really news. Who is he?—I'm most intrigued."

"He's a reporter on the *Record*—his name's Paul Scobie. Lesley dropped a flowerpot on his head when he was pestering her for an interview, so of course they got friendly!"

"Do you know what he's like?"

"Oh, he's very presentable—not at all my idea of a reporter. Actually, I persuaded her to bring him along here for a drink one evening—I thought I might as well encourage them all I could."

"I'll say! Do you think there's any chance that she'll marry him?"

"I think there's quite a good chance, if only she can get you out of her system. He's very determined."

"I certainly hope she does."

"Yes, darling, it'll salve your conscience, won't it? I still think it's quite wonderful the way you swallow the camel and strain at the gnat."

I let that pass. "I suppose I'll have to see her again after all that's happened, boy friend or no boy friend."

"Oh, I'm sure she'll want to see you. I don't think she'll be able to settle down at all until you've had a talk together."

"Well, I'll disengage myself as quickly as possible and leave the field clear for him."

"That's right, my sweet, but not *too* quickly—you don't want to make your relief obvious. After all, when she last heard from you three weeks ago you were practically suicidal over her."

"I know," I said. "That's one of the things I've got to clear up."

Chapter Twelve

When I left Isobel in the early hours I took away an armful of newspapers that she'd kept for me during my absence. I was in no condition to do anything about them that night, but after breakfast next morning I told the porter I wasn't seeing anyone, took my telephone receiver off the hook to stem the flow of congratulatory messages that had begun to pour in, and set to work to wade through the file. I found it absorbing.

It was the *Record*, apparently, that had first mentioned my disappearance. I couldn't discover just how they'd learned that I was overdue at the office, but from that point onwards the trail was well marked. They'd made inquiries at my flat, talked to the night porter, got hold of Lesley's telephone number, called on her, and been told about the telegram from Berwick. They'd then published an item saying that some anxiety was being felt about me. Next day the other papers had taken up the story, and the search had started. There were interviews with the sleeping-car attendant on the train and with the post office girl at Berwick. There were lots of pictures of me, mainly dating back to the war, and descriptions of what I'd been wearing when I'd last been seen. Next came reports from local correspondents saying that all trace of me seemed to have been lost from the moment I'd sent the telegram. So far, there was no suggestion of anything sinister. The accent was on my disturbed emotional state as revealed by my message to Lesley, and fears were obviously being felt for my safety.

Then, after a short lull, came the first reference to M.I.5 activity. Lesley had been visited by security officers, and further inquiries were being made in the Berwick district. These reports had been followed almost at once by the Admiralty statement about the missing documents—and that had really set things humming. It had emerged that I had been dissatisfied with my job and had shown some traces of left-wing leanings, and the telegram had been reinterpreted. The fact that I had had no known business in Berwick and that I didn't appear to have left the place by road or rail was linked almost immediately with the departure of the *Jan Sobolski* on the day of my arrival. A statement by an Electricity Board employee that he'd seen someone very like me strolling near the dock that morning had provided the final bit of evidence. My chain of clues had worked precisely as I'd intended.

At first, I noticed, the story had been handled with some caution even by the newspapers. Most of them had begun by treating it as a mystery, with lots of question marks and an avoidance of direct accusation. Then, when a nationwide hunt and checks at other ports had failed to produce any fresh information, they had moved by competitive stages to the open assumption that I'd departed for one of the Russian-controlled countries. Once they'd reached that point, they'd let things rip. They'd dug up every scrap of personal background stuff. They'd combed their library files, and they'd approached everyone who'd known me at all well. My noble, and now even more distant, relatives had all refused to talk, but they'd been written about and photographed and built into the story all the same. The fact that I was well connected had obviously been of major interest. Everything had been grist to the mill—one paper had even collared a small niece of mine coming out of school in Cheltenham, and had interviewed her on "Uncle Clive." The Cowleys had been drawn into it, and Walter Cowley had said he couldn't understand how a fine chap like myself could have done such a thing and the only possible explanation was that I was a sick man!

It was on Lesley, naturally, that most of the papers had concentrated. As far as I could see, no one had succeeded in getting a single word out of her after her first mention of the telegram, but they'd managed pretty well without. They'd photographed her leaving her flat, entering the clinic, walking in the park, shopping—one paper had even published a picture of her lighted bedroom window! They'd interviewed the charwoman who cleaned for her, and a waiter at one of the restaurants where she and I had dined, and an old school friend who'd once been away on holiday with her. They semed to have trailed her night and day, and to have pried into every corner of her life. I felt pretty indignant, until I suddenly remembered that I'd deliberately provoked them into doing it.

In addition to the background stuff about me, there were columns of speculation about my motives and discussion about my character. Most of the interest seemed to have centered on what the commentators called my Jekyll-and-Hyde personality. I was the patriot turned traitor, the hero rotted by postwar neurosis, the leader of men turned weakling. Along with the dissection came the editorial comment—and some of the leading articles were savage. It was the old story—the venom was all the greater because the villain had once been a public idol. Of course the more sedate dailies had managed to keep aloof from the hurly-burly, and even in the popular press there were one or two discordant and skeptical voices. They didn't amount to much, but what they'd said was interesting. One correspondent had remarked that, with the cold war beginning to thaw, I'd chosen an odd time to transfer my allegiance—though another had immediately replied that "peaceful coexistence" didn't mean that either side would be in any the less need of information about the other's weapons. A retired naval man, whom I knew slightly, had drawn attention to the fact that submariners were always hand-picked for their emotional stability and *esprit de corps*, which made my defection all the more astonishing. A member of the public had thought it strange that a man who apparently considered his work valueless should have bothered to take secret documents about it to a foreign country, while another had pointed out that according to the police I'd left virtually my entire wardrobe behind me, which was a curious thing for anyone to do who was setting out for Russia! But the general view was that neurotics were unpredictable anyway, and minor doubts had been swept away in the broad torrent of abuse. A statement put out by Moscow Radio denying that they knew anything whatever about me had just about clinched the matter.

In the few days before my reappearance, the more sensational papers had excelled themselves. Having supposedly turned my back on my country, I was evidently considered fair game for any attack, with no holds barred, and my private life had been completely torn apart. The article in the *Courier* was a real stinker and made me out considerably more of a libertine than I actually was, which was something of an achievement. A girl named Mollie Haven, with whom I'd had a brief and—as I remembered it—quite pleasant affair, had been persuaded to talk freely about me, and from what she said she'd evidently found me less attractive in retrospect than she'd appeared to do at the time. I wondered, ungallantly, what they'd paid her! A little somberly, I reflected that while I'd certainly achieved my purpose in getting the papers to say scurrilous things about me, it had been at a rather higher cost in reputation than I'd foreseen.

I threw the *Courier* aside and paged quickly through the last of the heap. Quite suddenly, the story came to an end. The day the Admiralty had announced that the missing documents had been discovered, a deep reflective silence seemed to have fallen upon Fleet Street. I'd have given a lot to have been around just then!

Finally I turned to the batch that had come in that morning. I was back in the headlines, of course, and they were bigger than ever—but how different! Now I was the reinstated hero, the maligned victim of circumstance. There was flattering detail about my ordeal and endurance on the rock. In the descriptive accounts of the Megstone by the reporters who had visited it, I couldn't find a single jarring note. My story had not only been accepted everywhere without question—it had been confirmed on the spot by independent witnesses. It really did begin to look as though I'd got clean away with it.

Editorially, the papers were now backpedaling as hard as they could, and several of them had printed special panels of fulsome apology and regret. However, it was obvious that they couldn't entirely undo the damage they'd done me, which any jury must regard as considerable. I recalled that in my own lifetime there had been at least two big libel actions in England where damages of £25,000 had been awarded, and looking back on them I couldn't feel that the defamation had been anything like as serious as in my case. I didn't see how there could be any effective defense, either. Reckless statements had been made about me on insufficient evidence—that would be my line—and the fact that the B.B.C. and the more sober newspapers had been careful to report the affair without directly accusing me of anything would make it all the more difficult for the less sober to offer any excuse. I couldn't see a paper like the *Courier* even attempting a defense—it would probably be only too happy to settle out of court. Probably they'd all be glad to settle if my claims were reasonable. In fact, if I now decided to go ahead with the second part of my plan, a very comfortable fortune appeared to be within my grasp.

Chapter Thirteen

Coping with callers and messages kept me fully occupied for the rest of the morning. The telephone rang incessantly, and telegrams came pouring in from all over the place—one of them, excitedly worded, from Walter Cowley, who had apparently heard the news in Brussels. I hoped he wouldn't come rushing home to shake me by the hand! Apart from the messages, there was still a steady trickle of inquiries from the papers, mostly about my plans for the future. There were several requests for signed articles, a suggestion that I should write a book about my experiences, and a proposal that I should give an interview on TV. In each case I said I'd have to consult the Admiralty about it.

Around twelve I rang Lesley at the clinic, since she was evidently leaving it to me to make the first move. By now, of course, she'd read the whole story, and I could tell she'd found the news quite overwhelming. I'd never heard her so subdued. I cut short the difficult exchanges and told her I very much wanted to see her. She said she'd be at home that afternoon, and I arranged to drop in at three.

It was a horribly self-conscious meeting, with both of us under severe strain. I was preoccupied with playing out a role I'd never liked and wasn't really fitted for; and though I could only guess at Lesley's feelings I knew they must be pretty complex. My gaunt appearance didn't make things any easier—she was obviously aghast at the change in me. For that matter, I wasn't too happy about the change in her—she looked as though she hadn't slept properly for weeks. It unnerved me a bit.

We sat down. I said, "It was decent of you to see me, Lesley, after all that's happened. I'm still not sure I oughtn't to have kept away, but I felt I had to see you just once, if only to tell you how very sorry I am about everything. I blame myself terribly."

"I don't know why you should do that," she said. "After all, you could hardly help getting stuck on a rock."

"I could have helped behaving like an adolescent. If I'd shown the slightest bit of restraint, none of this would ever have happened. The way I treated you that Friday was unforgivable, and rushing off as I did was idiotic."

"If that was how you felt," she said, "it was understandable."

I shook my head. "I'm deeply ashamed of myself. . . . You must have had an unspeakable time."

"I suppose we both have."

This wasn't getting us very far. Somehow I'd got to break the ice, but it showed no sign of shifting yet. I said, "What happened, Lesley? How did it all start?"

"A man came round from the *Record*—Paul Scobie. . . ."

"Oh—the man you threw the flowerpot at!"

For the first time, she smiled. "You've been talking to Isobel, have you? I didn't throw it at him—I was leaning out of the window, sort of threatening him with it, and it fell onto his shoulder. But that was the second time he came—the first time he merely called to ask me if I knew where you were. I was a bit worried because of the telegram, and I'd rung your flat and your office and been told you weren't back, and when Paul said that you ought to have been I got *really* worried—I thought perhaps something had happened to you. Paul said his paper might be able to help find you if they knew where to start looking, so I showed him the telegram—and that was the beginning of it all. After that, the newspapers never let me alone."

"I'm truly sorry."

"Oh, it wasn't as bad as all that. I did begin to feel rather like a criminal when I discovered they were following me about the whole time—some of them obviously thought I'd known all about what you were going to do from the beginning and intended to join you later. It was too fantastic!—and I got rather angry when one of the photographers came right into the clinic to get pictures. But I was frantically busy most of the time, and people were very kind. The doctors and nurses, of course—and the Cowleys, too, they were wonderful. Walter was sweet. And Paul's been a great help. . . . People are really a lot nicer than you'd think from reading the newspapers."

I said, "I'd like to meet Scobie—he seems to have made a great impression on you."

"I dare say you will—he's got into the way of looking in here quite often."

I nodded. "You know, I think what I'm most sorry about is that stuff the *Courier* printed about my—affairs. I'd have given anything to keep that out. It must have been dreadfully humiliating for you."

"It wasn't very pleasant."

"I never told you about them, because—well . . ."

"Oh, Clive, you don't have to explain them. . . . Good heavens, they happened before you met me. Anyway, I always assumed you'd had lots of girl friends."

"I was never quite as promiscuous as the *Courier* suggested."

"To be absolutely honest, I'm not sure my chief feeling wasn't one of envy! It sounded as though you'd had much more fun with them than you had with me."

"I felt differently about you. . . . Ah, well, there it is! There are lots of things I could wish undone—but they can't be."

She gave a little nod. "I've some regrets, too. After all, I believed what they wrote about you. Not at first, perhaps—but I did in the end."

"Everybody seems to have—it is a little depressing. But I certainly can't blame you. On the evidence, I don't see how you could have helped it."

"We'd been close friends—I ought to have had more faith in you, and not been so ready to jump to conclusions. I feel ghastly about it now. But when I remembered how restless you'd been over your work, and the things you'd said about Russia, it did seem just possible that you'd gone off there. I never believed you'd sold secrets for money—I told the security people you couldn't possibly have done that—but I did think you might have gone there out of frustration. The worst part of it all was that I thought it was my fault."

"Yours?"

"Why, yes. The way I worked it out, you couldn't possibly have made up your mind to go until that Friday, because you had just asked me to marry you again, so it looked as though it had all depended on me, and if I'd said 'Yes' you'd never have gone and everything would have been all right."

"You'd have been very foolish. Considering how I behaved, you did the only possible thing."

"No—I could have been less definite. I ought to have realized the state you were in—I ought to have been more careful. That was what I thought afterwards."

I smiled. "Well, you don't have to worry about that any more. As I never had any intention of going to Russia, you obviously didn't drive me to it!"

"No," she said. "I still find it all rather confusing."

"I don't wonder—I'm afraid I've been a great trial to you all along. That's something I want to talk to you about, Lesley. I shan't be giving you any more trouble—I can promise you that. I had a lot of time to think while I was on that rock, and I realized I'd been very selfish and caused you an awful lot of unhappiness and that I was a hopelessly erratic person who probably oughtn't to marry anyone, least of all a young girl who'd got her whole life in front of her. In fact, I realized you'd been absolutely right about us all the time, and that it would have been much better if we'd simply stayed good friends. I hope that's how it's going to be from now on."

She didn't say anything at all for a moment. I felt I'd made an effective little speech, and waited confidently for her comment. Then, for the second time in our acquaintance, she behaved unaccountably. As I gazed at her, tears slowly gathered in her eyes.

"I don't know what to say," she murmured. "I—I like you very much. You know that."

I hurriedly passed a handkerchief to her. "You like me, Lesley, and I like you, and that's fine, but—let's face it—as far as you're concerned, that's as far as it goes. You don't love me—you've made that perfectly clear. You may feel a little differently today, but that's because you're upset—and no wonder! The shock of all this business would upset anybody. Tomorrow you'll be your normal, common-sense self."

She dabbed her eyes and tried to smile. "I don't think I know what *is* normal where you're concerned. Sometimes I think you're quite impossible, but sometimes . . . Oh, I'm so mixed up. Things have gone so stupidly wrong with us, almost from the beginning, and I've never known why."

"They'll be better from now on. You'll be able to depend on me as a friend, and you'll find somebody much more suitable as a husband—someone who'll really make you happy."

She gazed at me in a forlorn sort of way, as though she didn't believe it and wasn't sure she wanted it.

"I still don't understand you," she said. "I'll *never* understand you."

"Sometimes I scarcely understand myself. I'm a bit of a case, you know. I probably need a psychiatrist, not a girl friend. . . ."

"The way things are going," she said, "I'll probably soon need one myself."

"Oh, nonsense!" I got up, trying to hide my exasperation. I knew I hadn't handled her very skillfully—the meeting hadn't gone at all as I'd intended. We were ending on a note of uncertainty, which was quite wrong. The trouble was, of course, that for a solid half hour I'd appeared a consistent and reasonably decent human being, the sort of man a girl *could* marry, which was almost unprecedented in our relationship. I hadn't meant to—it had just happened. Perhaps because I did genuinely like her, and felt guilty about what I'd done to her. Now the only way to end the thing was to be explicit, to tell her flatly that I no longer had any desire to marry her. That would send the trembling scales down on Scobie's side with a bump. But I remembered Isobel's warning about tapering off, and restrained myself.

"Look," I said, "have dinner with me soon—say, the day after tomorrow. By then, we'll both be feeling much more rational about everything."

"Perhaps," she said. "Anyway, it's a nice idea."

Chapter Fourteen

I spent some more time with Isobel that night, and I told her about Lesley's disquieting behavior. She wasn't surprised, and she didn't seem in the least perturbed. She refused to accept that I was in any sort of predicament. All I had to do, she repeated, was to exercise a little patience and withdraw from the scene gradually, and Scobie would do the rest. I still didn't feel too happy about things myself, but her faith in Scobie was reassuring.

She asked me if I'd made any move about the libel writs, and I said I hadn't actually done anything yet but after going through the pile of papers she'd given me I couldn't see any reason why I shouldn't. I gave her my layman's view of the prospects, which she found most encouraging. We also discussed an idea of mine that I should see a Harley Street man—not about my general health, which was steadily building up to normal, but about the nervous state I would say I was in as a result of all the unpleasant things that had been written about me. My idea was that I would complain of anxiety and sleeplessness and tell him that I couldn't face the prospect of going back to my old job, or indeed of taking any job, and try to get a sympathetic report out of him that would help the claim for damages. Isobel was in favor of anything that might boost the damages, and she said that she'd see that I looked sleepless.

I went through all the papers very carefully next morning, just to make sure that no danger signals were flying. I needn't have worried. For the first time in weeks, I was scarcely mentioned. The story was as good as dead, which was what I'd been waiting for. Now I could call my lawyer, Frank Malleson, and make an appointment with an easy mind. But there wasn't any great hurry, and I decided to do a couple of other jobs first. One of them was writing to Benson to explain how I'd come to strand his boat. He'd certainly have heard some part of the story on the radio, but I felt he was entitled to a letter as well.

I'd just about finished it when the phone rang. Rather to my surprise, it turned out to be Paul Scobie. He said he was speaking for himself, not for his office, and that he'd very much like to see me on a personal matter. I hadn't much doubt what that was, and I rather welcomed the opportunity to get on terms with him. I suggested he should come round that morning.

He arrived a little before twelve, and when I saw him I understood better why Isobel hadn't been very disturbed about Lesley. He was a tall, well-built man of about thirty, dark-skinned in an open-air sort of way, with a strong face and lively, intelligent eyes. I wouldn't have called him handsome, but he was very prepossessing, and if I'd really been a rival of his I'd have been seriously worried. As it was, I quite took to him. The feeling evidently wasn't mutual, for he shook hands with me as though he would gladly have dispensed with the formality. In the circumstances, I could hardly blame him.

"Have a chair," I said amiably. "I've been hearing a good deal about you from Lesley Ashe."

"It's about Lesley that I want to talk to you," he said, and continued to stand.

"I rather thought so. . . . Look, what about a drink before we start?"

"No thank you. . . . I've asked her to marry me."

"I see," I said, and waited.

"We became very friendly during your absence. She thought, of course, that you'd gone out of her life forever. Then you came back."

I gave a sympathetic nod.

"I wouldn't like you to get me wrong about this," he went on, after a moment. "I haven't come to plead with you on my own account. But now you're back she simply doesn't know where she stands. She's in a frightfully unsettled emotional state, and she could easily be heading for a breakdown. Things can't be left as they are. Somebody's got to clarify the situation, and I've given myself the job. In short—do you want to marry her yourself, or not?"

I was tempted to resent his direct manner but decided I'd gain nothing by it. He wasn't, I told myself, being deliberately offensive—he was simply a young man in love, driven to forthright speech by an overmastering concern for his girl. I doubted if he could be deflected. He certainly couldn't be browbeaten. He struck me as a man of caliber—the sort of man that in other days I'd have been glad to have as my Number One in a tight spot. Well, I was in a tight spot, all right, but he was on the other side, and I didn't feel very happy about it.

I said, "There's no question of my marrying her. She's consistently refused me."

He regarded me with cold anger. "That's no answer! As a matter of fact, I don't think she would refuse you now—not if you behaved like a normal human being. The trouble is, you don't. She's told me a little about your relationship, and it's the oddest I ever heard of. First you're crazy about her, then you cool off, then you deliver an ultimatum out of the blue and send her a melodramatic telegram that wasn't in the least necessary, and when you come back you're suddenly content to be a kind uncle to her! What way is that to treat a girl? Do you wonder she doesn't know whether she's coming or going?"

I didn't at all care for that speech. I didn't like the way his mind was working, with his talk about an odd relationship and an unnecessary telegram. It suddenly became clear to me that I wasn't going to have time to taper off after all—my hand was being forced. Hostile probing into the past by someone deeply interested in Lesley could be dangerous, and must be stopped. The only way to stop it, I thought, was to give the fellow the answer he wanted to hear, in as diplomatic a manner as possible.

"Look, Scobie," I said, "I'll be the first to admit that I haven't been much good to her. We haven't been much good for each other. When an older man falls for a young girl, it isn't all plain sailing, you know. For a time, I scarcely knew whether I was coming or

97

going myself. Well, I'm through that now. I can't undo what's done, but I'm quite clear about my own position. I don't think I could make her happy, and I've given up any idea of marrying her. All I'm concerned with now is what's best for her. If you want to marry her, and she likes you, good luck to you both!"

I thought I'd put it rather well. I thought that my renunciation would soothe and disarm him, and that he'd depart in relief and stop bothering about me. But my words had quite a different effect—they seemed to stimulate his interest in me. Perhaps his reporter's training had made him more than averagely curious about the way people's minds worked—or else there was something more that I didn't know about. Whatever it was, I found his intent gaze most disconcerting.

"You're certainly an extraordinary man," he said at last. "The way you've behaved, I find it hard to believe you ever really wanted to marry her."

I had to make an effort to keep my expression under control. At all costs I mustn't show anger or alarm over that particular remark. I mustn't appear to take it seriously at all. It had been thrown out in frustration and bitterness—it couldn't, surely, have any deeper significance? Still, I was shaken.

I said quietly, "I consider that a piece of impudence, Scobie, but as you obviously feel very deeply about Lesley I suppose I must make allowances. Shall we end this discussion? I assure you you've nothing more to worry about as far as I'm concerned, and that should satisfy you. I'm out of the picture."

"I wish that were true," he said. "Unfortunately, it's not as simple as that. You meant a great deal to her—far more than you seem to realize—and she's still got you deep in her system. What's happened lately hasn't helped, either. She's sorry for you because of the bad time you had, she admires you because of the way you stood up to it, and she feels guilty because she didn't believe in you. That's a pretty strong combination. That's why I tell you quite frankly that you've only got to go ahead to win. I wouldn't have a chance. *I* haven't been maligned and misrepresented, *I* haven't starved on an island, *I* haven't got a hollow, interesting face and a story of fortitude to tell. I'm just an ordinary bloke, not a re-established hero."

"That's all temporary," I said. "Her attitude will change."

"It may—but I'm not sure. It won't if you go on playing fast and loose with her."

"I resent that."

"It's a fair comment. You still plan to see her, don't you?"

I hesitated. Again my hand was being forced. But I'd already gone far in appeasement, and if I stopped now I should lose all the benefits of my earlier gesture. I gave a little shrug, and said, "I asked her out to dinner because—well, because she seemed unhappy and I didn't want her to feel we weren't going to be friends any more. Perhaps it was a mistake. I can easily excuse myself and call it off—and I'll do that. I'll leave the field absolutely clear for you."

He gave me a last curious stare and picked up his hat. "You know, Easton," he said, "it baffles me how a man could be so crazy about a girl and then pass up his chance when it comes."

He didn't shake hands again. He just went out.

Chapter Fifteen

I'd fully intended to phone Malleson before lunch, but instead I phoned Isobel. I said if she wasn't going to be busy that afternoon I'd like to drop in, and she said she wasn't. I waited till about three and then walked round to the house. She was looking very gay and attractive in a new frock that suited the summery weather, and she greeted me lightheartedly. We went into the drawing room, and I told her at once of my exchanges with Scobie. I said I particularly hadn't liked his remark about finding it hard to believe I'd ever wanted to marry Lesley, and that the whole trend of the conversation had rather disturbed me.

Isobel showed no sign of being disturbed herself. "The trouble with you, darling," she said, "is that you're over-sensitive where Lesley's concerned. I really can't see anything to be uneasy about. It was quite a natural remark for Scobie to make, after all."

"Was it?"

"I think it was. He's obviously very jealous of you, and it couldn't have done his self-esteem any good to discover you were ready to throw away something that he desperately wanted. In fact, he must have found it most galling—and he said the nastiest thing he could think of, which was that you'd never been serious. I don't suppose for a moment there's anything more to it than that—by now he's probably forgotten all about it."

I wasn't so sure. "Don't forget," I said, "that his parting shot was very much on the same lines. He seemed to me to be rather dwelling on the theme. He said he was 'baffled,' but I had the impression that he was intrigued and—well, suspicious!"

"Oh, darling, that's absurd—you must be imagining things. What on earth could he suspect?"

"That there was something phony about my relationship with Lesley."

She was silent for a moment. "Well, yes—he might think that—but he certainly couldn't *know*. In any case, does it matter?"

"It might matter if he started groping around for an explanation."

"Why should he bother?"

"He's a newspaperman, Isobel—it's second nature to him. Besides, he's gunning for me personally."

"I'd have thought he'd be fully occupied from now on consolidating his position with Lesley."

"That's just it. If he could hit the bull's-eye where I'm concerned he'd consolidate his position pretty effectively."

"Yes, darling, but he doesn't know that—and anyway he could never do it. He hasn't a thing to go on. You don't imagine he's going to say to himself, 'This man was a phony with Lesley so he obviously got himself stuck on that rock deliberately so he could sue the newspapers'!"

"There's quite a gap, I agree."

"Quite a gap!—why, it's enormous!"

"It won't be so enormous if I start issuing writs. There's nothing like the knowledge of money at stake to give shape to vague suspicions."

She laughed. "You'll certainly have to see that Harley Street man, darling—you really *are* suffering from anxiety! Actually, the risk couldn't be tinier."

" 'A cloud no bigger than a man's hand . . .' " I said grimly.

"Anyway, we've no choice but to take it."

"We have a choice," I pointed out. "We can still call the whole thing off."

"Don't be absurd."

"Well, now's the time, you know, if we're going to. We haven't tried to swindle anyone yet—if the whole truth came out tomorrow, we could still say we only did it for a laugh. We'd get away with it, too—nobody could prove we hadn't. But we've about reached the point of no return—once we sue for damages, everything will be different."

"Different—and better!"

"That's what we hope, but it could be different and worse. Not to put too fine a point on it, we'd have been guilty of conspiracy and attempted fraud and probably a lot of other things as well. You do realize, don't you, that if we were found out we'd be jailed?"

"Darling!—what a revolting idea!" She looked so taken a back that I could only conclude she'd never given it a thought before.

"It's better to be revolted now than surprised later," I said.

"Well, I refuse to discuss it—it's too idiotic. . . ." She gave me an angry, incredulous look. "You don't *really* want to back out now, do you?"

"Of course I don't want to. I can see a case for it, that's all."

"Well, *I* can't. Heavens, look at what we've been through—we've practically earned this money! Look at all the planning and the work, and how you nearly starved to death, and all the other frightful things that happened to you. Not to mention me almost killing myself on that drive! Honestly, Clive, I think you're crazy. We're as near as two people could be to getting hold of a very snug little fortune without making any more effort at all, and you talk of flinging it away because—because a jealous rival wasn't very nice to you! Really!"

"There's a little more to it than that," I said. "When we planned all this, it never entered our calculations that there'd be a newspaperman around afterwards, deeply interested in Lesley and hostile to me. We thought that Lesley would quietly fade out of the picture—but instead of that, Scobie's come into it. He's a new factor, and I have a hunch he could be a troublesome one. That's all."

"Well, I have a hunch, too," said Isobel, "and I feel that everything's going to be all right." She had turned pale, and her usually drawling voice had an edge to it that I hadn't noticed before. "I think it would be absolutely insane to drop everything now, and I won't hear of it. After all, I am in this, too—I did arrange about the bottle and get you out of your jam, so I have a right to a say in what we do. Haven't I?"

"Certainly."

"And I say we should carry on. It's the chance of a lifetime—the chance I've been waiting for for as long as I can remember. We know we want each other more than anything else in the world—and in a few weeks or months there'll be no more difficulties. We'll be free to travel, see all the places we want to see, relax in the sun—do everything we want to do. No more silly Admiralty, no more projects, no more being pushed around—no more tiresome Walter! And we'll be *together!*" She leaned towards me, putting on her most seductive air. "Clive, you don't *really* want to give me up, do you?"

I laughed. "Who's saying anything about giving you up?—You know damn well you're a microbe in my blood . . . ! No, I had a hunch and I had to tell you about it—that's all. I still think there may be something in it, but I could be wrong. Anyway, I've said my piece. I'm prepared to risk a gamble if you are."

"Darling! Then you'll definitely see your lawyer right away?—no more postponements?"

"I will if you're sure you want it. I'll ring him when I get back. . . . All I hope is that you fully realize what you're doing."

"Of course I do."

"There's an old Spanish proverb—at least, I think it's Spanish. . . . 'Take what you want from life—take it, and pay for it.' "

"What about it?"

"It's always been a favorite of mine—practically my whole philosophy. I'd like to feel that you shared it. I wouldn't want you to blame me later if anything went wrong."

"Oh, don't be so morbid, darling—nothing will go wrong. We'll pull this off if it's the last thing we do."

"It may be," I said.

Chapter Sixteen

The day the libel writ was served on the printers, publishers, and editor of the *Courier*, I jumped right back into the news. There wasn't much the papers could add to the bare announcement, but that didn't prevent them from telephoning me and sending their reporters round to see if I'd any comment to make. I referred them all to my solicitor—all, that is, except Paul Scobie. When he rang up from the *Record* and said he was speaking for the paper and could he come round and see me for a few minutes, it seemed a good chance to find out how things were going, so I said he could.

I soon came to the conclusion that Isobel had been right about him, and that we hadn't any further cause for anxiety. His manner was still reserved, but he no longer appeared actively hostile. I got the impression that he was prepared to let bygones be bygones, and I concluded that he must be making progress with Lesley. I felt glad about that, for her sake as well as for my own. I asked politely how she was, and he replied with a faintly ironical smile that she was improving. He'd certainly mellowed.

It didn't take long to dispose of his business. He said he didn't imagine I'd want to talk about the writ, and I said that was a realistic approach. He asked me if there were likely to be any more writs, and I said it was quite possible. He nodded, and said the view in Fleet Street was that I was going to pick up a lot of money in damages. A few days earlier I'd have shied at a remark like that, but there was no hint of an *arrière-pensée* in his tone, and I wasn't worried. He went on to ask me one or two general questions—about my health, which I said wasn't too good, and whether I planned to do any more sailing, and whether *Shelduck* had been salvaged yet. I told him I didn't think she had, and that it might be a tricky business getting her off, and we talked a bit about the Megstone. I hadn't realized it before, but it seemed he'd been one of the reporters up at Seahouses when I'd given my press conference, and he'd spent the best part of a day on the rock. He appeared to have enjoyed his visit.

"We got some quite good pictures," he said "Some of them have been published, of course, but not all. Perhaps you'd care to see them." He produced a sheaf of prints from his pocket and gave them to me.

I looked through them with interest. They made up a pretty complete record of my stay on the rock, and they stirred some lively memories. There were several of *Shelduck* on the ledge, taken from various angles. There was an interior view showing where the planks had been stripped, and there was one of the broken petrol pipe, and there were others of the pile of limpet shells, the empty tins, and the distress signal on the summit. Incongruous among the pictured relics was a beautiful close-up study of a guillemot in flight.

Scobie, glancing over my shoulder, explained. "Bill Cranston— that's the chap who took the pictures—is a keen amateur ornithologist. He was really more interested in the birds than in the story—it was all I could do to tear him away from the place."

"It's a nice piece of work," I said. I turned over a few more of the prints and came to one of some scattered debris on the top of the rock. It was the remains of my fire, though at first I scarcely recognized it. Someone had evidently been poking about among the ashes, and I asked Scobie about it.

"Oh, we all did that," he said. 'We were interested in the various things you'd used for fuel—they helped to build up the story. . . ." He pointed to the next print. "That's an intriguing one."

I looked at it. It was a close-up of the fissure in the rock surface near the summit, with the broken cormorant's egg clearly visible at the bottom.

I said, 'What's intriguing about it?"

"Well, the crack was immediately underneath your big bonfire. We uncovered it when we moved the debris."

"Oh, yes?" I still didn't get it.

"We thought it was a bit odd, because we remembered you'd told us there weren't any eggs around when you first got to the rock—which was when you lit the fire, of course!"

I felt as though a depth charge had exploded under my hull.

"Well, I certainly didn't notice any," I said, in as casual a voice as I could manage. "I must have overlooked this one. Pity!—I could have used a nice boiled egg at that stage."

"According to the experts up there," said Scobie, "cormorants don't lay their first eggs in the islands before May, even in a very warm season."

I forced a grin. "This must have been a precocious bird."

"Yes—my friend Cranston thought it was pretty precocious. In fact, he was quite excited about it at first—he talked of sending in a report to the Ornithological Society. But then we managed to scoop up the remains of the egg, and we saw we were wrong. It was actually quite fresh—it couldn't have been there more than a day or two at the outside."

"Fascinating . . .! I suppose the bird must have burrowed through the ashes and laid the egg in the crack underneath."

Scobie shrugged. "I have it on the best authority that cormorants don't burrow through ashes and lay their eggs in cracks! It's certainly most peculiar. . . ." He looked hard at me. "Can *you* think of any explanation?"

I gave a short laugh, as though the topic were too trivial to discuss further. "No, I'm afraid it's not my line of country at all."

"Ah, well . . ." Scobie moved towards the door. "Perhaps Cranston will have some more ideas."

I said, "You're forgetting your photographs."

"Oh, you can hang onto those, Commander. As a memento of your—extraordinary adventure!"

Chapter Seventeen

Well, there it was! My earlier uneasiness about Scobie had proved after all to be only too well founded. My moment of complacency over his change of mood had been stupid wishful thinking. Not only was he gunning for me harder than ever, but thanks to an appalling oversight on my part he'd picked up what promised to be some deadly new ammunition. If his temper appeared to have improved, it was merely because he felt that everything was going his way.

I poured myself a stiff whisky and sat down in a pretty grim frame of mind to assess the damage.

Although Scobie hadn't put his latest accusation into words, I had little doubt what was in his mind. The chain of logic was complete, and the conclusion, however startling, was inescapable. That egg—that confounded egg!—had been laid before the fire had been lit. But it hadn't been laid until May—so the fire hadn't been lit until May. And if I'd delayed lighting the fire until May, while falsely asserting that I'd lit it in April, the obvious deduction was that I'd had some powerful—and presumably discreditable—reason for not wanting to disclose my whereabouts earlier.

The next step, for a man of Scobie's worldly experience, was only too clear. He'd ask himself what I could have hoped to gain by deliberately remaining concealed on the Megstone in conditions of considerable discomfort and some danger—and it wouldn't take him long to work that one out. With my libel writ just filed and Fleet Street buzzing with forecasts of big damages, the answer would surely stare him in the face. I'd stayed in order to cash in. He'd be bound to realize, too, that I'd done more than merely grasp the opportunity provided by a chance stranding and an unexpected outbreak of public suspicion. He'd know that no serious accusations had been made against me for at least a week after my disappearance; that during the first few days, certainly, I couldn't possibly have gathered from my radio that I was under suspicion. If, therefore, I'd failed to take the obvious step of lighting a fire during those first few days, it could only have been because I'd foreseen the situation that was going to develop and had planned to exploit it. That, inevitably, pointed to a premeditated, put-up job.

I wondered how far Scobie had already traveled along that logical road, and it seemed to me that it must be quite a long way. As I cast my mind back to the first conversation I'd had with him, I realized that he'd probably been groping even then towards a theory. He must have known about the egg, and though at that time he might not have ruled out some remarkable ornithological explanation, the even more remarkable alternative could well have been in his mind. His comment about my unnecessary telegram rather suggested that—and of course my renunciation of Lesley would have fitted perfectly. As I saw it now, he'd been piecing things together and weighing the evidence all this time, and had shown his hand only when my libel writ had seemed to clinch the matter. Even then, he hadn't accused me—he'd left it open to me to offer some explanation about the egg. He was evidently a cautious as well as an angry man. It was a formidable combination.

If I was right, his task from now on would be comparatively simple. It had always been basic to my plan that no suspicions should arise—and if it hadn't been for that damned cormorant they wouldn't have arisen. Now that they had, every past action of mine would fit his theory, and all he needed to complete the jigsaw was patience and persistence. I could have done it myself, in his place and with his knowledge, so why should he fail? He would note the remarkable coincidence of the mislaid documents; the careful secrecy of my trip in *Shelduck*; the strangely sudden signs of neurosis in a hitherto apparently stable character. He would certainly fasten on my convenient change of clothes in Berwick, and possibly on the equally convenient fact that I'd left my dinghy behind. Above all, he'd read into my treatment of Lesley the contradictory attitudes of a man who was using her as a tool—and resentment would charge him like a dynamo. As I mentally reviewed the prospects, it seemed to me almost certain that in a matter of days Scobie would be after me again with a comprehensive indictment.

It was a pretty black situation, and I could see only one faint ray of hope. However skillfully Scobie built up his case, he would scarcely dare to spread his suspicions around unless he could prove it in the legal sense—and that might be very difficult. So far, there was only one really damning piece of evidence—my failure to light the fire. For all my other actions and attitudes, I had plausible reasons. The circumstantial case against me would no doubt be impressive, but as long as I had an alternative explanation for everything, which couldn't be disproved, I could count on the law's protection. Everything turned, therefore, on the fire. Somehow I had to think up a reasonable, noncriminal explanation of my delay and subsequent deception—something which, however bizarre, could be made to sound feasible.

I thought about it for a long time, but I didn't make any progress. In the end, I decided to tell Isobel what had happened and see if she had any ideas.

Chapter Eighteen

Now that I was under suspicion, it no longer seemed safe for me to go round to her house. Scobie, the trained sleuth, would be quite capable of keeping a watch on my movements, and the last thing I wanted was to start him wondering about Isobel too. From now on, I decided, when she and I had to meet, it must be in some place too remote for successful trailing and where there was no likelihood of our being seen together. I knew a spot that would do perfectly—a thickly wooded hilltop above a disused quarry a few miles out in Surrey, not far from where I'd lived as a boy.

I made no attempt to explain the position to Isobel over the phone. I simply told her that there had been an unpleasant development and that I had to see her, and she was sufficiently worried not to argue about my arrangements. We drove out of town separately, making visual contact at Croydon according to plan, and from there on I acted as pilot. On the quiet Surrey byroads there was no difficulty about making sure we weren't being followed, and the quarry itself was quite deserted. I turned in along a well-remembered track through the trees and came out on a stretch of short downland turf, bounded by a two-hundred-foot chalk precipice that was unprotected except for a few "Danger" signs. It wasn't the sort of place that anyone would choose for a picnic, and I felt sure we shouldn't be disturbed. I parked my car among the trees, and then I walked back and joined Isobel.

"Well, what's happened?" she asked sharply.

I got in beside her and broke the news. I told her about Scobie's visit, and the egg, and the deductions he must have drawn. I said I thought it wouldn't be long before he arrived at the truth, even if he hadn't done so already, and I told her why. She heard me out in tense silence.

"Well, this is a fine mess!" she said at last.

'I'm afraid it is."

"Surely you should have realized what might happen? You knew the egg was there."

"I should have, I suppose, but I didn't. At that time I wasn't thinking of anything except lighting the fire and getting off the island. I was in a fairly bad way, you know."

"Yes, yes, I know," she said impatiently. "Don't start being pathetic now, though—it's a bit late in the day."

I stared at her. This was a new Isobel, a stranger to me. She was looking away, remote in her concentration, the lines of her face hard.

"Anyone can make a mistake," I said. "I won't pretend I expected anything like this to happen, but I did my best to warn you the other day that something might go wrong."

"I know you did, but you only said you had a hunch—you didn't tell me you'd already made a ghastly blunder. I thought at least I could rely on you not to do that."

"Well, I'm sorry," I said.

"A lot of good that's going to do us! My *God*, you've let me down!"

The speed and venom with which she'd turned on me were an eye opener. I felt my own temper rising, and I had to make an effort to control myself.

"Look, Isobel—recriminations aren't going to get us anywhere."

She seemed not to hear. "I can tell you this—if I'd thought for a moment you could be so idiotically careless, I'd have taken your remarks about going to prison a lot more seriously than I did!"

"There's no need for you to worry about that," I said coldly. "The way things are working out, you're not in the picture, and with any luck you won't be. Naturally, I shan't bring you into it. If anyone goes to prison, it'll be me."

There was a significant pause.

'Well, I wouldn't want that either," she said, after a moment—but her face had begun to clear. "After all, I did let you do it—almost encouraged you, in fact. It wouldn't be fair. . . ." Her mouth slowly curved in the mocking smile I knew so well, and she added, "Of course, I'd visit you regularly!"

"Thanks!"

Her hand crept out, seeking mine. "I'm sorry, darling. Did I seem to nag? I didn't mean to—it was just the shock after all, you *had* set a pretty high standard for yourself, hadn't you? You've practically conditioned me to expect perfection from you. Anyhow, I'm sure we'll find some way out. Let's sit and think seriously about this fire business. . . ."

I felt too sick with her to do any serious thinking myself, and waited in glum silence. I didn't have to wait long.

"I know," she said. "Couldn't you say there'd been a misunderstanding and that you'd actually lit *two* fires in different places, one at the beginning and one just before you were rescued? That would account for the egg—it would be under the second one!"

I shook my head. 'It won't do. I told the reporters at the press conference that I lit a fire the first night at the top of the rock—it's all in the record. And there's only one lot of ashes there."

"Couldn't the other lot have been washed away in the rain?"

"There'd have been traces—a fire leaves its mark for months. Besides, if I'd really lit a second fire, I'd have told Scobie so straight away when he mentioned the egg—and I didn't. . . . No, the only hope I can see is to think of some convincing explanation of my actual behavior. *Why* didn't I light the fire at the beginning, and *why* did I say I did? If we could answer those two questions satisfactorily, we might still be able to bluff our way through."

"Yes—I see. . . . It's not very easy, is it? I suppose it wouldn't be enough to say you'd been rather glad to be there at first—you know, because of the peace and the solitude—so you hadn't in fact made any immediate attempt to get off, and then at the end after all those horrible things had happened to you it had seemed too incredibly silly so you'd pretended you'd lit the fire right away?"

"I can't imagine anyone believing it," I said. "Not in the light of all the other evidence, particularly. I know I was supposed to be pining for a lost love, but only a lunatic would have chosen that place. It was too damned uncomfortable."

Isobel became silent again—but only for a moment. Suddenly she grabbed my arm. "I've got it, darling, I've got it! Your mentioning your 'lost love' gave it to me. It's a wonderful explanation. . . . Don't you see, you'll have to say it was all because of Lesley. Everyone knows you were in a terrible state about her, so it'll be quite easy. When you got stuck on the rock you realized she'd be bound to worry about you, and you decided to stay there as long as possible in the hope that when you did finally return she'd be so relieved she'd fall into your arms. After all, she probably would have if you'd wanted her to—and it's just the kind of thing a neurotic would think up."

I gazed at her in awe. In a hundred years, I'd never have thought of anything so novelettish.

"And naturally," she added, "you wouldn't have wanted to admit it, would you? In fact, it's not an explanation you'll want to use at all unless you have to."

"That's an understatement," I said.

"All the same, darling, if it's a choice between appearing a complete cad and stitching mailbags, it's surely much better to appear a cad?"

She certainly had a point there. I sat quietly thinking about her proposal, and it seemed to me that I might just about get away with it. It showed me in such a very bad light that even Scobie might hesitate before ruling it out!

"There is one snag," I said. "I've already told Lesley that I had lots of time to think on the island and that as a result I underwent a complete change of heart about her. How can I square that with having deliberately stayed on until the eleventh hour so that she would worry about me? It would seem an incredibly sudden change of heart."

"But that's just how hearts do change, darling—in a few hours. Everybody knows they're unaccountable things. And certainly nobody could possibly prove that yours didn't."

"Well," I said grudgingly, "it's something to fall back on if I can't think of anything better."

"You may never need it at all. I wouldn't be surprised if you're overestimating Scobie's cleverness."

I didn't reply to that. I knew I wasn't.

Chapter Nineteen

The next few days were grim. I longed to get the showdown over, but there was nothing I could do to hurry it up and not much I could do to prepare for it. In the meantime I had no job to occupy me and certainly no inclination to amuse myself. The thought of meeting old friends and colleagues and probably having to talk about the Megstone was more than I could bear. I repulsed all advances on the plea that I was ill. I was suffering badly from reaction after all the excitement and felt pretty jaundiced about everything. The prospect of wealth and freedom with Isobel had become far too uncertain to afford me any consolation. Besides, my feelings for her had begun to curdle. I suppose I'd known all along that she would be just a fair-weather mistress, and up to a point I'd accepted that. I had no reason to expect anything else. All the same, her outburst of self-centered fear and anger at the quarry had come as a shock. Not even an allure like Isobel's could compensate for viciousness and unreliability in a tight spot. I very much doubted now whether I *wanted* to go away with her. I felt quite relieved that, for the moment, I didn't even have to see her. It was bad enough having to listen to her facile assurances that all would be well, drawled out each night over the telephone. Optimism without courage wasn't going to be any help at all. Her voice, which I'd once thought so attractive, now grated on me harshly.

Then, on the morning of the fourth day, the tension broke. I'd just finished breakfast when the porter rang to say that Paul Scobie was downstairs asking to see me. If the idea was to throw me off balance by a sudden appearance, it failed to work. I knew exactly what I had to do. My tactic was to behave naturally and convince him that he was wrong—and I was all set to do it. I said he could come up.

He looked, I thought, a bit worn. He refused the cigarette I offered him, but this time he did sit down.

"I expect you know why I've come," he said.

"No, I can't say I do. . . ." I smiled. "Unless it's to tell me that you're engaged to Lesley?"

He studied me for a moment in silence. Then he said, "It's no use, Easton, the act's wasted on me. . . . You know, and I know, that you stranded yourself on that island deliberately so that you could collect from the newspapers. I have to hand it to you—it was a brilliant plan. The mistake you made was to bring Lesley Ashe into it. I'm afraid that's going to be fatal for you."

I stared at him. "Would this be your idea of a joke, by any chance?"

"I was never more serious in my life."

"Then you must be off your head . . . ! Good God, man, do you realize what you're saying? I've a damn good mind to throw you out."

"That's up to you. If you do, I shall have no choice but to go to the police."

I continued to stare at him for a second or two. Then I threw out my hands in a gesture of helpless bewilderment. "You intrigue me so much, Scobie, that I suppose I'll have to listen to you first and throw you out afterwards. . . . Just what *is* this nonsense you've got into your head?"

He told me—in great detail. It turned out precisely as I'd expected—he'd used his brains, he'd made a few inquiries, and he'd fitted the pieces together perfectly. His case was almost exactly the case that I'd marshaled against myself. He started with the egg—and he finished with the egg. He spoke confidently, but there was no hint of triumph in his voice—if anything, his manner was rather quiet. I heard him out in fascinated silence.

"And you really believe all that?" I said at last.

"I see no reason not to."

"It's incredible!—absolutely incredible! . . . You do realize, I suppose, that there's such a thing as criminal libel and that you can be sent to prison for it?"

"Yes. I'm taking a calculated risk."

"Then there's something very wrong with your calculations! Why, it's the most malicious bit of fact twisting I ever heard in my life. . . ." I broke off. "What's behind it, Scobie? Surely you haven't cooked this up because you think it'll help you with Lesley Ashe . . . ?"

He gave me a wry look. "Even *I* know more about women than that!" he said. "I haven't even dared to tell her what I've been doing. As I said before, she liked you a lot. If I'm proved right, and you come to grief, I shall get no thanks from her. That's really why I wanted to talk to you first, instead of going straight to the police—at least she'll know that I gave you a fair chance to answer the case. Even so, I'm afraid it'll take me some time to live it all down!"

"Then why are you doing it?"

"I'm not a very forgiving chap. What you did to Lesley was infamous, and I'm not going to let you get away with it."

I considered for a moment. Then I said, "Look, Scobie, I'm going to be perfectly frank with you. By pure chance, you've been able to build up a circumstantial case against me that looks quite impressive. I admit that. But you've only done it because you've allowed yourself to be blinded by your prejudices. Every single fact you've mentioned has a perfectly innocent explanation, and I'm willing to spend time convincing you of that. The alternative is to break you—and, if only for Lesley's sake, I don't want to have to do that. I'd sooner try to make you see sense before it's too late."

"Go ahead," he said, "I'm listening."

I went ahead. I covered all the ground that he'd covered, and it took a long while. It was hard to judge what effect I was having on him, but from time to time he gave a little nod, and that encouraged me. I dealt with his charges point by point, and disposed of all but the main piece of evidence. I left that till last.

"As for the egg . . ." I said—and hesitated. Hesitation, I knew, would seem called for when I was about to confess to a particularly despicable bit of conduct—but there was more to it than that. Now that the moment had come, Isobel's explanation stuck in my throat. I'd almost as soon have shown cowardice on the bridge before a young officer as let Scobie hear that contemptible tale. Jail would at least be clean! I decided, suddenly, that I must try to bluff it out.

"The fact is," I said, "I know nothing whatever about the egg. All I can say is, it's a very remarkable thing." I paused, and added meaningly, "Very remarkable indeed . . . ! Oh, don't misunderstand me—I'm not suggesting for a moment that you put it there yourself—though considering how you disliked me, and what there was at stake, a jury might wonder! What I do suggest is that it might well have got there by accident while you fellows were on the rock. You told me yourself that you were all poking about among the ashes, and someone could easily have kicked it down the crack."

I waited. There was a risk, I knew, that he might have been the first on the scene that day, that he might have found the egg before anyone else had had a chance to get near it. But if he had, he didn't say so. He seemed rather to be turning my suggestion over in his mind, and I decided to follow up my advantage. I'd suddenly thought of an entirely new argument, and a powerful one.

"In any case," I said, "what you seem to be forgetting in all this is that I damn nearly died! A few more days, and I'd have been too weak to move. Do you seriously think I'd have marooned myself on a rock two miles off shore when I couldn't be certain of being rescued?"

"Oh, but you could," he said quietly. "There was the bottle."

"The *bottle!* Why, that was a chance in a thousand. It could have drifted out to sea, or smashed on a rock and sunk, or been washed up in some remote spot—I certainly wouldn't have dared to count on it. It was a miracle that it was found at all."

His reaction wasn't in the least what I expected. "Yes," he said, "*I* thought it was a bit of a miracle, myself. In fact, it struck me as so extraordinary in the circumstances that I went back to Bamburgh to make some more inquiries. Young Alan Granger is still up there, and I had another talk with him. Nobody thought to ask him, before, just how he happened to find the bottle—it didn't seem important at the time. Well, I did ask him. It appears that he didn't just stumble upon it by accident. His attention was drawn to it—and in a rather strange way. A woman came up to him and said she'd seen a big crab. In fact, there wasn't a big crab—but there *was* the bottle, with the message plainly visible inside. It seems odd, don't you think, that she didn't notice it herself and pick it up?"

"Now what are you suggesting?"

"I'm suggesting, Easton, that you had an accomplice who planted the bottle by previous arrangement—and that that's why there was a miracle."

I felt pretty sure then that the duel was lost—he had too many concealed weapons. But I struggled on.

"This gets more and more fantastic," I said. "I suppose I also arranged that it should be a warm sunny day, instead of a typical English one, and that a boy should happen to be playing on the beach so early in the season? Do you really suppose I would have trusted my life to such a chance?"

"I think you must have. After all, you hoped for a big prize—and the gamble wasn't so terrific. A day or two more or less could hardly have mattered to you, as long as you knew you were going to be rescued in the end. There was bound to be a fine day, and a child playing around there, sooner or later."

If I hadn't been in such a jam, I'd have found the situation funny. For the first time, he was wrong in a major detail of his reconstruction—and it made no difference! I could hardly tell him that I'd actually planned, if all else failed, to save myself by swimming!

"Well, I find it difficult to keep pace with your imagination," I said. "The whole thing's just too preposterous. . . . Look, is there any chance of finding this woman? Was the boy able to describe her?"

"Not very exactly, I'm afraid."

"That's a pity. If we could produce her you'd soon be brought to your senses. . . . As it is, we seem to have reached a deadlock. I don't see how I can disprove your ridiculous theory—and you certainly can't hope to prove it."

"I think I can produce her," he said. "There are one or two pointers. You see, if my theory's right and you did conspire with a woman, she must be someone you've seen a fair amount of lately, because of all the planning you'd have had to do. An intelligent woman, naturally. A woman you felt you could trust, a woman you were close to—a mistress, perhaps. An attractive woman."

"You'll find," I said, "that that doesn't narrow the field as much as you might think!"

"Perhaps not, but there's something else that does. As I see it, your whole plot depended on your getting to know a girl whom you could pretend you wanted to marry and send an ambiguous telegram to. Lesley Ashe was the girl. I asked myself how you came to meet Lesley Ashe. Well, you met her at a party at the Cowleys'. She'd never been asked to the Cowleys' before—and Isobel Cowley had had nothing to do with her for nearly a year. It was an invitation out of the blue. I'm wondering if that introduction was entirely unpremeditated."

"Of course it was, you suspicious fool!"

"I don't think so. And I don't think *Walter* Cowley has been the attraction for you at that house all these months. . . . There's one other relevant point, by the way. At the time when the bottle was found, Walter Cowley was already abroad, so Mrs. Cowley was free to come and go without anyone knowing about it. I think she went to Bamburgh."

"So now you're prepared to slander Isobel Cowley too!"

"I'm prepared to stake everything," he said, "on a meeting between her and the boy. If Alan Granger says she wasn't the woman on the beach, I'll be through. You'll be entitled to my head on a charger. If he says she was, the case against you will be complete, and *you'll* be through. If Isobel Cowley won't agree to the meeting—well, then it'll be up to the police."

It sounded a bold gamble, the way he put it, but I knew he was safe. The boy might fail to identify Isobel from her appearance, but he'd be bound to remember that distinctive voice of hers.

Perhaps he'd already mentioned the voice—perhaps that explained Scobie's assurance. I thought it rather likely.

There was nothing to be done now except play for time. I lit a cigarette and got to my feet. "Well," I said, "this at least is something that can be settled—provided Mrs. Cowley doesn't mind humoring a lunatic! Why don't you give her a ring and ask if she'll see you?" I picked up the telephone receiver, and passed it to him. "The number's Flaxman 04302."

For the first time, I thought I caught a flicker of doubt in his eyes.

"Go on," I said, "test your crazy theory."

He took the receiver and dialed the number. We stood listening to the burr-burr at the other end—but there was no reply. It was an anticlimax for both of us.

"Oh, well," he said, "I'll call her later."

"You'd better order that charger, too!" I told him. "You're going to need it."

It wasn't a bad curtain, I thought, even if I *was* ringing it down on myself.

Chapter Twenty

I called Isobel's number every fifteen minutes for the next two hours, and just before twelve I got an answer. I gave her the gist of what had happened in a few terse sentences and urged her to leave the house again right away. For all I knew, Scobie might decide to drop in on her without warning as he'd dropped in on me, and I didn't want him to see her before she was fully briefed. We arranged to meet at our old rendezvous in the country, and I hung up.

I drove out of town in a somber mood. I'd done my best to keep Isobel out of it, but I'd failed, and I didn't expect any gratitude for trying. She was a woman, I now knew, who went solely by results, and if last time was anything to go by I could count on a pretty hot line in recrimination. It wasn't even as though I had any very hopeful suggestions to make. As far as I could see, we'd been left with almost no room for maneuver. Virtually, the game was up.

I reached the chalk pit ahead of her, but it wasn't long before I heard her engine. As soon as she'd pulled in among the trees I joined her. She didn't look too good. She'd slapped fresh make-up on in a hurry and her lips were a crude slash in a pale, tense face. Her "Hullo!" was as friendly as a dagger thrust. I got in beside her and gave her a cigarette. Then I told her, in detail, everything that had passed between Scobie and me; and I said that I thought a meeting with the boy would finish us.

I was prepared for an outburst at the end, but none came. I suppose she'd had time to condition herself a little on the way down. She sat rigid behind the wheel, one white-knuckled hand still gripping the rim. She was scared, all right, but she showed no sign of panic. In fact, her deep frown suggested concentration, not weakness, and I began to hope that in this final crisis she might prove less of a handicap than I'd feared.

She was still inclined to clutch at straws, though. "Isn't there a chance," she said, "that you may be exaggerating the danger? Surely the evidence of a child couldn't really make so much difference?"

"I'm afraid it could make all the difference. Without it, Scobie has a theory that he can't prove. With it, he'll have a complete case."

"But the boy might be making a mistake. How could anyone be sure?"

"Scobie would be sure—sure enough to bring in the police. And they'd check up in other ways. They'd check your movements that day."

"I don't see how. We went over all that when you came back. . . ."

"We went over some of it—we forgot the obvious thing. You must have bought petrol on the Great North Road."

"Oh! Yes, of course. . . . Four or five times."

"There you are, then. They'll almost certainly find a garage hand who remembers you or the car."

She gave a little nod and was silent for a while. Presently she said, "I'm just wondering if *I* couldn't do something with Scobie. If I put on a really good act and said the whole thing was too ridiculous and it was a pure waste of time for me to see the boy—would he in fact go to the police . . . ? I thought I made rather a hit with him when we met—we certainly got on very well together. . . ."

"You'll find the magic has worn off," I said. "He knows too much now. He'd be bound to take your refusal as a confession of guilt."

"And if he told the police, would they make me see the boy?"

"They'd do more than that—they'd probably stage a full-dress identification parade, with a lot of other women repeating the sentence you spoke to young Granger—and that would be that!"

"You seem very certain of everything."

"It's no good shirking the facts."

She jabbed her cigarette savagely into the ash tray beside her. "Well," she said, "you got us into this mess so now you'd better get us out of it. What do you suggest we do?"

That sounded more like the authentic Isobel! Her tone was so venomous that I was tempted to tell her I didn't care what she did, but I decided that it wouldn't be very constructive. I said, "There seems to be only one thing for it—if we want to keep our freedom, we'll have to clear out."

"Run away, you mean?"

"Yes."

"Where to?"

"That'll need thinking about.... We might fly to South America—it's where most fugitives seem to go to."

"Couldn't we be brought back?"

"Not easily. There are one or two countries we don't have extradition treaties with—I seem to remember Brazil's one of them. Anyway, if we kept on the move it would be a difficult job to catch up with us."

"What would we live on?"

"I've got enough to pay our fares and keep us for a few weeks. After that, I frankly don't know. I suppose we'd have to try to find some work."

"It's a glittering prospect, I must say!"

"We're hardly in a position to pick and choose. It's the best we can hope for at the moment."

"Well, it's not good enough. If you think I'm going to abandon everything I've built up here and spend the rest of my life washing dishes in some filthy dump in Brazil, you're making a great mistake."

"Then what *are* you going to do? You might just as well try to see things straight for once. The alternative to clearing out is jail. Six months or a year, I'd say, even for you. Perhaps more. We'll be arrested directly Scobie produces the boy, and there isn't a thing that can stop it."

Isobel's face had turned a blotchy white. "There must be—there's *got* to be! I couldn't *stand* it. . . ."

"It probably wouldn't be as bad as you think," I said. "In fact I'm not at all sure that for you it wouldn't be the better choice. If I'd got away to South America, they'd have to be lenient with you. Why not pay the price and start again? At least when you came out, you'd be in the clear."

"In the clear! In the gutter, you mean . . . !" Her voice shook with sudden hate and fury. "My God, why couldn't Scobie mind his own business?"

"He thinks it is his business."

"If only there were some way of keeping him quiet! He's the only one who's thought this out—it's in his head, but in no one else's. Without him, we'd be quite safe—do you realize that?"

"Well, he's hardly likely to fall under a bus to oblige us."

"Some men in your position would give him a push."

"I dare say, but I don't happen to be one of them. I may be all sorts of things, but I'm not a thug."

"I'd have thought it was a bit late for fine moral distinctions."

"Everyone draws the line somewhere. I draw it at murder."

"You weren't always so particular."

"What on earth do you mean?"

"You must have murdered hundreds of people in that submarine of yours. Innocent people who'd done you no harm. Women and children, too, I wouldn't be surprised."

"I doubt that. Anyway, it was war."

"Isn't it more sensible to kill one person for a good private reason than hundreds because someone else tells you to?"

"You're talking nonsense," I said. "This is getting us absolutely nowhere. . . ."

"It could easily get us where we want to go. The simple fact is that if Scobie's allowed to tell his story, we're finished. If he's prevented, we haven't a thing to worry about. We'd even get the money!"

I stared at her. "Isobel!—you can't be serious about this?"

"Would it be so very surprising if I were? You must know by now that I'm not exactly an angel."

"If I thought you were really trying to talk me into killing Scobie," I said slowly, "I think I'd call it a day and take you to the police myself!"

For a moment she gazed at me with unfathomable eyes. Then she shrugged and reached for a cigarette. "Well, there's no need to excite yourself," she said contemptuously, "I wasn't serious."

"I'm glad to hear it. I was beginning to wonder."

"Theory and practice are hardly the same thing, are they? Heavens, we're in enough trouble already without that...."

"Then we're back where we were. What are you going to do—stay and face the music, or come with me?"

It was a long time before she replied, and when she did her tone was surprisingly indifferent. "Oh, I suppose I may as well come with you," she said.

Chapter Twenty-one

Before we separated, we agreed on the things that each of us must do. Isobel was to return home and wait there until Scobie got in touch with her, which he was almost certain to do before the day was out. When she saw him, her line was to be that his suspicions were fantastic, but that if it would set his mind at rest she had no objection to meeting young Granger—provided she herself didn't have to make any effort in the matter. That would disarm Scobie temporarily, and we would probably be able to count on two or three days of immunity while he made the rather tricky arrangements to bring the boy to London. Isobel would ring me as soon as she'd seen Scobie, to give me a rough idea what sort of timetable he was working to. Meanwhile, I'd get on with our own escape plans.

I gave her ten minutes' start on the road and then set off after her. I didn't hurry, for I had a great deal on my mind, and it wasn't all to do with the uncertain future. My thoughts kept drifting back to Isobel's horrifying suggestion about Scobie. It *might*, of course, have been just a wild idea which she'd never intended me to take seriously, but somehow it hadn't sounded like that—not at first, anyway. I had an uneasy feeling that she'd been doing a bit of reconnaissance and had drawn back only because she'd met resistance. Suppose I'd given her the green light?—would she have drawn back then? I rather doubted it. I'd known for a long time that she was a very determined woman where her own interests were concerned; now it seemed possible that she was also a dangerous one. I might be misjudging her, but after that sinister conversation I wasn't prepared to gamble on it. I knew at last, with certainty, that our association must come to an end. I'd see her settled somewhere if I could, but after that she'd have to fend for herself. I was through with her.

My thoughts switched to the problem of how we were going to leave the country, and I soon realized that it wasn't going to be quite as simple as I'd supposed. There'd be no difficulty for Isobel—she could book her passage and fly off anywhere without causing the least commotion—but I wasn't so sure about myself. There seemed a very considerable danger that if I booked in London for a trip to a place like South America, some newspaper would get to hear about it and print a paragraph—and at the first hint of flight, Scobie would be certain to call in the police and have me stopped. It might be safer, I thought, if I sent Isobel off first, and then slipped over to France by steamer and booked an air passage there. I'd be much less likely to attract unwelcome attention that way. There'd be a currency problem, but with my full allowance of traveler's checks and a bundle of smuggled sterling in my pocket I should just about be able to manage. In any case, it seemed the smaller risk.

As soon as I got back to town I called at my bank. I told the assistant manager, with whom I was on good terms, that I was thinking of going off to the South of France for a holiday during the next day or two. I said it was going to be a bit of a rush, and I asked him if he could make out the checks right away to save me another visit. He seemed quite happy to do that for me. I also cashed a check for a hundred and fifty pounds in fivers, saying something about having a lot of shopping to do. I thought it might seem unusual for anyone to draw so much cash at one time, but he showed no surprise. He merely wished me a pleasant trip. Back at the flat, I made sure my passport was in order and stuffed it into my breast pocket with the money and the checks. The feel of the bulge was most reassuring.

I spent a busy afternoon on the telephone, making anonymous inquiries at several travel agencies about fares, flights, and sailings to various South American countries. By the evening I'd collected all the information I was likely to need. I went out for a drink at my local pub and took the opportunity to cash a check for ten pounds. Just to be on the safe side, I cashed another at the garage where I usually got my petrol. I returned to the flat about seven. I asked the porter if there had been any calls for me, but there hadn't. I settled down again with my pile of jotted notes and worked out a provisional plan which with luck would get the two of us to Rio de Janeiro before the storm broke.

There was still no word from Isobel, and by eight o'clock I was beginning to feel slightly worried. If Scobie had delayed so long in getting in touch with her, after all that he'd said, it looked as though he might have changed his plans—and any change was likely to be for the worse. . . . In the end, I rang her up.

There was no reply. I thought I must have made a mistake over the number and dialed again, but there was still no reply.

I couldn't understand it. If she'd already seen Scobie she ought to have let me know, as we'd arranged. If she hadn't, she ought not to have left the house. . . . Unless, of course, she'd gone off to meet him in some other place. . . .

Some other place!

It was fantastic, I knew, but I suddenly thought of the chalk pit! A picture, preposterous but vivid, rose in my mind—of Scobie standing near the edge of the cliff, and of Isobel solving all her problems with one quick movement!

I was obviously getting jittery, and I tried to dismiss the picture—but I didn't entirely succeed. Hadn't she, that very moruing, suggested "giving him a push"? The chalk pit could easily have been in her mind. She was certainly desperate enough. As I looked back on our conversation, it seemed to me that the very suddenness with which she'd dropped the subject could have been the cover for a secret intention—to do the job without me and present me with an accomplished fact. It would be difficult for her, no doubt, to get Scobie out of town—but could the possibility be ruled out? She was very inventive, very persuasive—she might well have made up a sufficiently plausible story to get the eager Scobie out to a quiet rendezvous after night-fall. And once they were at the chalk pit, Isobel knew the terrain, Scobie didn't. . . .

It would be very tempting. All the more so because no one would think of associating Scobie with Isobel. They had met only once—there was no hint of anything between them. If his body were found at the foot of the chalk pit, she'd be about the last person the police would suspect. She'd imagine herself to be quite safe. *I* would know, of course—and I'd made my attitude very clear—but would that be a danger to her? With growing concern, I realized that if anything did happen to Scobie I'd be involved up to the neck. Literally! No one would ever believe that I'd had no part in the last act, when I'd plotted everything else with Isobel from the beginning. If Scobie were killed, I'd be forced to keep what I knew to myself—or hang. And Isobel would know that.

By now I was thoroughly alarmed. If Isobel hadn't talked as she had that morning, if she hadn't mysteriously disappeared instead of ringing me, the thought of anything so macabre as murder would never have entered my head. Now that it had, I couldn't get rid of it. I told myself there must be some other explanation, some simple explanation, but I couldn't think of any that adequately accounted for her silence. It certainly didn't seem at all likely that she and Scobie had gone out for a friendly drink together, considering the kind of thing he had to say to her. He'd have wanted privacy—and what better place could there be than her own home ...?

Well, there were ways of checking—negative ways! I rang the *Record* and asked for Scobie. They told me he'd been off duty all day and suggested that I should try his home. I looked him up in the book and there was only one Paul Scobie and he lived at Orpington. I hadn't much hope, but I rang the number. Almost at once the receiver clicked, and a familiar voice said, "Paul Scobie here."

I was so unprepared that for a moment I scarcely knew how to explain my call. Then I said that I was sorry to trouble him but I'd been wondering whether he'd seen Mrs. Cowley, and if so what had happened, and as she herself wasn't at home I'd thought I'd ask him. There was a brief silence, and then he said, yes, he had seen her, around five, and that she'd agreed to meet the boy. He didn't sound in a very expansive mood. I said, "Well, that's splendid," and made another crack about the charger, and rang off.

I felt absurdly relieved and slightly ashamed of myself. My fears had really been too fanciful. I could see now that Isobel would never have attempted to carry out, single-handed, the sort of feat that I'd been imagining. Apart from anything else, she'd have been much too concerned with her own skin to take the physical risk of trying to get a big man like Scobie over the edge. It just wasn't her line of country. But that left the problem of her whereabouts still unresolved—and now I felt more puzzled than ever.

I rang her number again, but there was still no reply. I couldn't begin to think what she was up to.... Then I suddenly wondered if by any chance she'd decided to clear off on her own! The possibility hadn't occurred to me before, but she might well have come to the conclusion that she'd be better off without me. She'd be less conspicuous, she'd be able to choose a more congenial place for her exile than South America—and on her own it was quite likely she'd soon find some man to take an interest in her.... Perhaps she was already on her way to the Continent.

Anything seemed better than waiting for news that didn't come, and presently I strolled round to her house to see if her car was in the garage. It wasn't. That seemed to knock my new theory on the head, because she couldn't possibly have taken the car abroad with her at such short notice and it would have been pretty pointless merely to drive it to the coast. It was all very strange. For a moment I stood hesitating in the drive. There might be some clue in the house, if only I could get in. ... I ran my eye over the front windows, but they were all securely fastened, and in any case there was still too much daylight for me to attempt anything so near the street. I walked round through the side gate to the back door. There was a high wooden fence blocking the view from the ground floor of the next house and only one upper window directly over-looking me—a bathroom window, I thought. I could see no sign of anyone there, and I tried the door. It was locked. Then I noticed that the kitchen window was unfastened. I took another quick glance up at the bathroom, pulled the window open, and went through it as though I were escaping from a fire. I stood listening for a moment, but no one seemed to have noticed me. I closed the window and set about searching the house.

I went through every room, but I didn't find anything helpful. There was no disorder, no sign of a hasty departure, nothing at all out of the ordinary. The cupboards in Isobel's bedroom were full of clothes; her suitcases were stacked on the shelves. I looked in her bureau, and almost the first thing I came across was her passport. I wondered if she might have left a message anywhere, but she hadn't. The whole place was just as it would have been if she'd simply gone out to the pictures for an hour or two.

Completely baffled, I returned to the hall. There seemed no point in waiting around, and I'd just made up my mind to leave boldly by the front door when I heard the sound of a car drawing up outside. I peered cautiously out of the narrow hall window, and there was Isobel's Sunbeam Talbot by the gate! So she'd decided to show up at last! I felt pretty savage with her, but at least I'd be spared anymore fruitless speculation. The car door slammed, and she came walking slowly up the path. I didn't want to scare her and risk raising a rumpus—it seemed wiser to retreat to the back and come openly to the front door after she was safely inside. . . . Then I suddenly froze. Behind the Sunbeam Talbot another car had pulled up—a big, black car with a "Police" sign above the roof.

There wasn't much time to figure things out. All I could think of in that bleak moment was that Scobie had fooled us—that he'd taken his story straight to the police after all, and that Isobel had been picked up and grilled. . . . Then her key was in the latch. There was no possibility now of retreat. I looked again at the police car and saw that neither of the occupants was making any move to get out. If I could stop Isobel giving the alarm from sheer fright, there might still be a chance for us. I stepped back behind the door as it opened. The moment Isobel was inside I clapped a hand tight over her mouth and heaved the door shut with my shoulder.

For the fraction of a second she struggled wildly. Then her rigid body relaxed as she recognized me, and I let her go. She leaned back against the wall, breathing hard.

"God, how you frightened me!"

"I was afraid you'd yell. Come on—we can't talk here."

I propelled her into the kitchen and closed the door. "Well, what happened?" I said.

Her lips moved, but she seemed unable to get any words out.

"For heaven's sake, Isobel, pull yourself together."

"I'm sorry. . . . I'll be all right in a minute. . . ." Her face was quite white, and she looked as though she were about to faint.

I stepped across to the cupboard where she kept the brandy and poured her a stiff shot. She choked a bit, but slowly the color crept back into her cheeks.

I waited.

"It's—not very easy," she said at last. "To tell you the truth, darling, I've a bit of a confession to make."

"Oh?"

"You see—after you left me I started thinking about the future and how ghastly it was going to be, and I realized I just couldn't face it. . . . I'm not strong and brave like you, Clive, and I simply *couldn't* give up everything here. You know the last thing I'd ever want to do would be to let you down, but you did say you didn't want me to get into any trouble, didn't you . . . ?" She gave me a pathetic little smile.

"What are you trying to tell me?"

"Well, darling, the fact is—I've been to the police. It seemed the only thing to do, I was so desperate. I drove round to the station and saw an awfully nice inspector and he took me to Scotland Yard and I told them everything—well, almost everything. As I say, I knew you didn't want me to get into trouble so I had to fib a bit about myself. I—I told them I'd only joined in with you for the fun of the thing, because you'd said it would be an amusing hoax, and that I'd never realized there'd be money involved and that I was horrified when I discovered what was happening—I mean about the libel suit. . . . Of course they asked me why I hadn't come to them straightaway, and I had to pretend I'd been too afraid. They thought I meant of you—imagine!—and that's why they sent the police car back with me, to protect me. I told them that *that* wasn't necessary. . . . Anyway, I'm sure my explanation went over all right because they didn't seem to think anything much would happen to me as I'd come and told them all about it of my own accord, so you see you won't have to worry about me any more. . . . Oh, darling, it must sound awfully mean, but it won't really make any difference to you, will it? and honestly I was in such an awful state. . . ." She broke off. "Well, for heaven's sake, *say* something."

I gazed at her, fascinated. It was all so completely in character that I knew I ought to have foreseen it. It scarcely seemed worth while to tell her what I thought of her. Contempt would have been wasted on her.

"I suppose," I said at last, "it hasn't even crossed your mind that I might tell a different story?"

Incredibly, she looked indignant. "Darling, that *would* be a beastly thing to do, and not a bit like you. After all, you did promise me that if anyone had to take the blame, you would—that was part of our bargain, wasn't it?"

"It wasn't part of our bargain that you should virtually hand me over to the police! I take it they've gone along to the flat?"

"I don't know. They did say they'd like to talk to you, so I suppose they might have. . . . Must you go back there?"

"By pure chance, no—but *you* didn't know that. You didn't even know that I'd left the place. You thought they'd find me there."

"If you mean I wanted you to be caught, you're absolutely wrong and it's horrible of you to suggest it. There just wasn't a thing I could do about it, that's all."

"I suppose they asked you about my plans?"

"Well, yes . . ."

"What did you tell them?"

"I said you were thinking of going abroad, but not immediately—I said we'd arranged to meet tomorrow to talk about it. So you see they're not likely to be in any desperate hurry about you."

I looked at my watch. It was just after nine fifteen. The night ferry would be leaving Victoria at ten, and if I didn't get that I'd be stuck till morning. I opened the back door and peered out.

There was a wall at the end of the garden and beyond that someone else's garden and another house. In darkness, getting through to the next street would have been child's play, but dusk was only just beginning to fall, and I couldn't afford to wait. Not more than a few minutes, anyway—then I'd have to risk it.

I turned to Isobel for the last time.

"There's only one thing I want to say before I go. You're not just a miserable little coward, Isobel—you're a fool. You think you're going to get away with this, don't you? You think you're going to be able to settle down again just as though nothing had happened. . . . Well, you haven't a chance. They won't send you to prison, but everything else will happen to you. Nobody's going to believe your story. Scobie knows damn well you were my mistress, and he won't keep that to himself. He'll go after you as he went after me, because of Lesley. You'll never persuade anyone that what you did to *her* was an amusing hoax. The newspapers'll tear you to shreds. By the time they've finished with you, you won't know where to hide yourself. Everyone will loathe you—and unless I'm very much mistaken, that'll go for Walter too. In your own graceful phrase, even a worm will turn—and I'd lay long odds that this is going to be the turning point. Believe me, I don't envy you."

She made no reply, and I left her. I left her without emotion, without a single significant thought. She was lovely, but I hadn't loved her. She'd betrayed me, but I found I didn't even hate her. I felt thankful the whole thing was over. That was about all.

I made my way quickly to the wall and peered over. There was no one in the garden beyond, but I could see a woman moving on the top landing of the house. It was still far too light for comfort, and I knew I should be horribly visible crossing the lawn if she happened to look out. But it was now or never, and I couldn't delay. Nerve and speed were my only hope. I heaved myself onto the wall and dropped lightly down on the other side behind a rhododendron bush. I could no longer see the woman at the window. I waited a moment and then dived for a lattice gate close to the back door. It creaked abominably as I opened it, and a dog started to bark in the house. I heard a man's voice telling it to be quiet.

I crept past the kitchen window, crouching low, strode down the short drive to the front gate, let myself out, and walked rapidly away. As I reached the end of the street I glanced back, but no one had come out after me. The first hurdle, at least, was behind me.

I spent several anxious minutes looking for a taxi, and by the time I reached Victoria it was nearly a quarter to ten. I quite expected a holdup over tickets, as I had no reservation, but I was booked through to Paris without any trouble. The Customs on the platform were a mere formality. I found a seat, and after the train had started I walked down the corridor and managed to organize myself an unclaimed sleeper. The *wagons-lits* steward showed me to my berth and collected my passport. "You'll get it back in the morning, sir," he said.

I hoped he was right—but I knew I couldn't count on it. It was possible the police were waiting patiently for me to return to the flat—but it was equally possible they had already alerted the ports. In a few hours, I might be in France or I might be in jail. I just didn't know which. I lay quietly on my bunk, trying to take a philosophical view, but it seemed an awfully long way to Dover—and once we were there, the waiting was even worse. Every footstep in the corridor set my nerves jangling. Every moment I expected to be hauled off the train. Then, at last, I felt the throb of the ship's engines and the first gentle heave of the sea, and I turned over and went to sleep.

In the morning I was in France—and I got my passport back.

As the train sped southward, I knew regret as well as relief. What I'd tried to take from life seemed pretty futile, now. It had cost me friends, career, reputation. The price was high. The outlook was obscure. Yet, as I thought of the days ahead, I felt the first stirrings of a new excitement. The future might well be grim—but somehow I didn't think it was going to be tedious.

www.ingramcontent.com/pod-product-compliance
Ingram Content Group UK Ltd.
Pitfield, Milton Keynes, MK11 3LW, UK
UKHW040105010325
455690UK00002B/21